SUPERNATURAL

HORROR STORIES

Real accounts of: Ghost Creatures, Demons and the Paranormal

ANN GAIMAN

TABLE OF CONTENTS

INTRODUCTION

Caution: If you are faint of heart, turn back now. This collection of stories will not bring you comfort or pleasant dreams. It will not soothe your mind or leave you content. Those happy thoughts are best left to other books. This is a much different anthology, one that peddles terror, panic, and dark truths. The accounts of real experiences you are about to read will make you question what lurks in the shadows. Did you lock your door? Are you sure you're really alone? Was that noise you heard really the wind, or was it something more?

Folklore stories change from one area to the next. They morph depending on the cultures that tell them and the people who are brave enough to share what they have seen. The whispered details conjure up images of everything from shapeshifters and demonic beasts to things that are felt but not seen. Sometimes the encounters are a whispered voice, a smell that seems out of place, or leftover shredded remains.

It is human nature to try and rationalize strange experiences, to comfort ourselves with rational explanations, but what happens when the explanation falls short?

There are things that even the most skeptical people can't rationalize away: that foreboding feeling when something unseen is watching you from the shadows, the clenched knot in your gut when you know danger is near, the indescribable animal instinct that urges you to run. Perhaps those sensations are left over from a time when humanity was all too aware that the dark was indeed something to be feared. The Survival instinct isn't something easily forgotten. Sometimes, that intuition is the only thing keeping you alive, whether you know it or not.

If you want to remain in the dark, stop now. If your gut is telling you that what you will read will change the way you look at the world, perhaps you should listen. The terror captured in these pages is not for everyone. A flicker from the corner of your eye will never again be just a figment of your imagination. The shadows in the corner of your room will never be truly empty. Every temperature change, every strange smell, and every bizarre encounter with a creature—some that seem human and some that do not—will make you question your safety and maybe even your sanity. The brave people written about in the following stories do not share these occurrences lightly. They have experienced what goes bump in the night—and most of them were lucky enough to live to talk about it.

Most of the people involved in these recounted events were never the same after their ordeals. Some have resisted telling others about their experiences out of fear or the worry of not being believed. For others, telling their stories is the only way to warn others about what is out there. You see, these cautionary tales are not just a compilation of fireside ghost stories and eerie folktales. They are a warning. It is up to you to decide if you will heed them or not.

 If you insist on reading further, you will not only be opening this book but also your mind. The words you read may haunt you, and after you read them, there is no going back. Afterall, even the most incredible stories contain a grain of truth—or as in the case of these stories, sometimes more. The folktales you are about to read will challenge your definition of impossible, and in the famous words of Albert Einstein, "Once you eliminate the impossible, whatever remains, no matter how improbable, must be the truth."

CHAPTER 1:

SCARY TRUE SKIN WALKER STORIES

Skinwalkers are known as animals that are possessed by people—or people that have the ability to morph between an animal and a person. Sometimes, the skinwalker falls somewhere in the middle, exhibiting both traits of a human and a beast. In Navajo tradition, skinwalkers are evil witches or *yee naaldushi* ("it goes on all fours" in Navajo) that take on the appearance of a wild creature. Sometimes, there is a motif involved, such as a coyote as a trickster or malicious one, or a crow as a bringer of misfortune. Generally, these beings are associated with bad omens, so they are best avoided. Such power isn't acquired by chance. To become a skinwalker, a Navajo medicine man or woman needs to reach the highest level of the priesthood and perform some truly evil deed, such as killing a family member. Once they have attained the supernatural powers of changing into animals, they are free to inflict suffering however they wish—following people around, tapping on windows in the middle of the night, and making scary noises to pierce the silence.

The shapeshifting ability is also associated with a flight-or-fight response. There have been stories of native witches transforming into a cat when cornered by people more powerful than them. Other abilities include the power to transfer their consciousness to another living thing—such that they can control the actions of the host. Once in animal form, the witch is granted supernatural physical ability, such as being able to travel long distances without getting tired.

It Watches Me

I grew up in a mostly white neighborhood in southern Utah. Though I am of mixed descent, I have a grandma who is full-blood Navajo who lives a few hours' drive away from us. Every once in a while, my dad drives me and my younger brother Joseph to her house to stay for a few days. The place is fairly remote—it's just a piece of desert land with a double trailer stuck in the middle. She has a chain link fence that separates her plot from her neighbors, but the distance between the two homes is astounding. In a way, I envy that way of living. You never have to see your neighbors or worry about them spying on you. I get a little weirded out every time we go because my grandma is the type of person who believes they are cursed. When grandpa passed away—I was still too young to understand—but the one thing I remember is how my grandma openly talked about "the curse" and how it killed grandpa.

My dad says that grandma is going senile, so we need to check up on her frequently. If she talks about weird things, we have to go along with it. We had a visit recently, where we stayed for Labor Day weekend. I was pretty bummed out about it because some of my friends invited me to a concert, but my dad said that visiting her was more important. He feared that she was developing dementia and that it was getting worse. When we got there, the yard was very unkempt. Weeds were growing everywhere, and my grandma had spread what looked like a white powder all around her house. My dad brought his lawnmower to help clean, while I and Joseph were tasked with entertaining her.

She was making food that day and told us we could watch TV while she prepared dinner. Though it was still light out, the inside of her trailer was completely dark. We had to turn the lights on because she kept them off. All of her windows were draped in heavy curtains that let zero sunlight in. It wasn't long before she started doing weird grandma things. She handed me a Coca-Cola bottle filled with a greenish liquid and said it was a protective ointment. It kind of smelled like flowers and rubbing alcohol. It didn't sting, though. I rubbed some on my hands and neck and did the same for Joseph.

I noticed that grandma kept peeking out of the curtains with wild eyes. My dad noticed it too and finally asked her what she was doing. "*Yenaldlooshi* is watching me," she said with a nonchalant tone. She could have been talking about the weather or today's Powerball numbers. My dad gave me a look that told me we had to be patient with her. This continued for the rest of the stay there. She would periodically look outside or open the front door and sniff the air—but never staying outside for a prolonged period. I thought it was a little scary, but as my dad said, we had to be patient with her.

When it was time to go back home, my dad threw open the grill and had a small barbecue just for us. I and Joseph took it upon ourselves to prettify the yard, so we planted potted flowers my dad bought and placed stones in interesting patterns. I don't know how this happened, but I lost track of my little brother Joseph. One second he was looking for stones right next to me, and the next second I hear grandma yelling at him from the porch. "Get away from that animal, Joseph! It isn't safe!" I turn around to see grandma with a bowl of casserole in her hand, and then I see Joseph sitting behind the chain link fence poking his fingers through the gap at some large dog. I know it was big, as Joseph is already large for a 3rd grader and yet this dog towered over him. It took a while to recognize that this dog wasn't at all normal-looking. The snout was longer than most breeds, the fur long and hairy like a wild animal. Then, I saw the sunlight reflect off its eyes—yellow as a traffic light.

But it wasn't staring at me or Joseph. It was looking directly at grandma with such intensity! I've never seen a dog stand perfectly still and stare like that. Normally, they move around or sniff at something after getting bored of just sitting there, but not this dog—or thing. Grandma was about to get up to retrieve Joseph when the creature let out a chilling snarl and bound off. My dad asked her if she knew the owner of that dog, and her reply was that of frantic screams. "The *Yenaldlooshi* has found me! The Yenaldlooshi has found me!" She yelled and clutched her chest. It took us a little while to calm her down, but when she did, she went into the house and produced a bowl of white powder that she proceeded to dump along the fence where we found Joseph and the dog. I will never forget the horror-stricken look on my dad's face when grandma started losing it. I will never forget the deep yellow eyes of the *Yenaldlooshi* or whatever it was.

My dad said it wasn't safe to leave grandma alone, so she had to come with us and sleep on the couch. My dad kept rifles in his house, so I felt much safer in being home. Doubtless, so did grandma, as she didn't once spread her white powder. She also brought along bottles of green liquid that she made us all splash on our backs each time we showered. My dad towed her trailer somewhere else after that and sold the land at a bargain price. Late at night, I could hear both of them at the dinner table discussing the curse and how a childhood rival was stalking her. It was difficult to follow because they talked in hushed tones, but I swear about hearing that a witch had cursed her—but what I wasn't sure was if the creature with yellow eyes was a minion of some sort or the actual witch. You don't ask such things around here.

A Friend of the Snow

It gets unbearably cold in the region of Northern Canada. It gets so bad in winter months that even cars won't start. My family has lived there for a while now, and we have grown accustomed to many of the hazards of the land. If we run out of food, we can readily hunt for deer or elk—not to mention the abundance of wild berries and nuts.

As a consequence, I grew up side by side with hunters. I got my first rifle at 14 and was allowed to go on solo hunting trips when I became 15—not the usual coming-of-age story, I know. When I was 18, I went on such a hunting trip—just me, my gun, and my knife. I crept out of bed early to see if I could find any rabbits following the previous night's thaw. It didn't take too long to find fresh prints, which I was an expert at identifying by now—two hours or so into the woods, and I noticed something strange. The usual woodland sounds were missing; no birds chirping about or the rustling of leaves. It was as if the wind just disappeared and the animals too. Maybe it was too cold for animals to be out? That wouldn't make sense, as the rabbit tracks were fresh.

The usual protocol for hunting rabbits involves following the tracks they leave as well as any droppings and waiting for them to appear. In that deafening silence, I couldn't hear anything. I laid in the snow for another fifteen minutes or so before deciding that no rabbits would be coming this way. I slung my rifle over my shoulder and dusted the snow off my jeans. When I turned around, I saw a large black dog looking directly at me. I jumped back, not expecting to see a thing. Upon further expectation, I saw that it had a collar and figured it had wandered off. The closest houses were about an hour away, so it didn't immediately click why this pup was all the way out here.

"Are you lost, buddy?" I said, hoping it was friendly—but the dog just stood there, staring at me. Something about its eyes made me uneasy. Something must be wrong with it because they had a milk film—maybe it was blind. Those eyes seemed to peer into my soul. I approached slowly, not wanting to startle it or come off as aggressive. I called out to it again, and it didn't so much as flinch—no wagging of the tail or puckering of ears. I managed to take out some dried deer meat from my bag and offered it to the dog, which took it and gulped down. I guess it was starved because it hardly even chewed. It took out some more and patted its head after it finished eating—not as aggressive as other dogs I've encountered in the wilderness.

A loud, menacing bark nearby made both of us turn around. A pack of maybe 6 dogs stood there looking at us, each with the same white film on their eyes. I was about to slowly reach for my gun to scare them away because boy, did they look mean. But as I lifted my hand, the dog from before licked my hand as to say "thank you" and went to join the others. The lick was icy, and it sent shivers down my spine. One of the dogs was visibly larger than the rest, and for a moment, its eyes lingered on me even when the rest of the pack had started to walk away. That really freaked me out, but I was relieved to see it turn around at last. I felt a little proud of myself for not jumping the gun, as it were. What a strange breed. I've never encountered those eyes in canines before.

As the pack left, life started to return to the forest. I could hear animals again, strangely enough. I thought little of it at the time because I heard what sounded like the squeaks of rodents nearby that I had to investigate. I killed three rabbits before heading home. Call it hunter's intuition, but there was something eerie about those dogs I saw. I only referred to them as dogs because wolves have lighter fur in this area. The occasional black wolf is rare, and even then, their eyes aren't like the ones I saw.

I asked my dad if he knew of any local dogs that fit the general description of what I saw. His answer made me feel uneasy because there was no other explanation. He told me there weren't many dogs around our area, and of the ones he knew didn't match my description. Weird. Did I encounter some ragtag pack of strays who somehow managed to live in the wilderness? The big dog that gave me a hard stare down before leaving was easily wolf size. It must have been 100 pounds, at least—about the same weight as an adult male.

Though I went on many more hunting trips by myself, I never saw the black dog or its pack out in the woods. The winter soon passed, and things got much warmer. More animals were out, which is always good for hunting. I was half-expecting to run into the black dogs any day because of the abundance of food and the lower temperatures. One spring morning, I heard scratching at the door and went to go see what it was. I thought it was just the rain, but sure enough, there was the same dog from before with wet matted fur. It had the same unmistakable eyes. I gave it a few head pats and fetched some more dried deer jerky, which the dog gulped down just as it had in our previous encounter. How on earth did it find me? Even if it were to follow my scent, the Spring rains would have long washed away any traces of it. Now, it knew where I lived. Though of course, back then, I thought nothing of it. The dog ate a bit more and then left. But I swear, it gave me a little bow at the end there as if saying thank you.

I was awoken in the middle of the night as if waking from a nightmare. My hearing rate was way up, and I'm not entirely sure why. I think some instinctual animal spirit inside of me was telling me to wake up because the danger was nearby. Immediately, I knew why. Beyond my window, there was a figure—just standing there by the tree line. I reached for my rifle just in case and took a peek out the window for a better look. But whatever fear I had dissipated as I stared outside, looking head-on at what appeared to be a native woman. It was dark, but I could tell she was naked. She had long black hair twisted into two braids and pale skin that shone in the moonlight. Above all, she had the same white eyes of the dog that ate my jerky. I was speechless. I didn't know what to do except for lowering my rifle. She noticed me and quietly started walking toward the window. She was actually coming towards me! I didn't know whether to panic or call the police. The funny thing is that I wasn't really scared, just shocked at the strangeness of it all.

She eventually got within a few feet of the window but didn't stop her pace. She was a woman, alright, probably in her early 30s or late 20s—young, but not too young. I jumped when she tapped on the window for me to open it up. I tried talking to her in English, but she didn't seem to understand. She only spoke some strange, ancient tongue that I didn't recognize. For a moment, we just stared at each other, seeing as we couldn't communicate with spoken word. Her eyes were magnificent but didn't look sick. The more I stared, the more I felt like I was in a dream. I saw galaxies swirling round and round—I saw the past, and I saw the future. Heck, maybe it was all a dream. But then, she caught me by the hand with an icy cold touch. My body temperature must have fallen by a few degrees. She closed my hand and left a white feather. Then, she bowed and ran off into the moonlight. I know it wasn't a dream, as the feather was still in my room the very next day. I have no explanation for what it was, but it was the most surreal thing I've experienced. I've never done drugs before, but that's what I imagine they would feel like.

I never did see the dog or the woman again. I still keep the feather around as a memento of the strange encounter. After doing some research, I knew what I saw. It must have been a skinwalker. The woman was probably a witch or priestess that for whatever reason decided to make me a friend. Sometimes, I find presents around the house or on my hunting trips—dead birds nicely rolled-up in leaves, nuts, and berries. I'm not one to let such good things.

CHAPTER 2:
REAL UNEXPLAINED CREATURE SIGHTINGS

In the realm of the paranormal, there is a subset of sightings that do not fall in line with any established facts. People have seen things that are inexplicable given the common set of knowledge learned through school and waking experience. It is no wonder that these sightings are often terrifying. How do you make sense of that which has no prior record of existence? These encounters go beyond the scope of ghosts and UFOs. There is a long list of cryptids, some of which are discussed in later chapters, that may pass as unexplainable phenomena to those who are unfamiliar with the literature. However, these creatures, upon being identified by an expert, will conform to the descriptions and attributes that are common in the cryptid literature—real unexplained creatures that have no source of reference. They are, in a sense, untold legends that may one day belong to the cryptid family if they are properly scrutinized.

Encounters that fall in this range vary, from unidentified land animals to anomalies of sky and sea. Sometimes, these things aren't real, in the sense that they lack objective truth. The mind is apt at simulating explanations that are fallacious. For example, a bag floating in a murky river may be mistaken for a sea creature of unknown origin. A regular animal that is common knowledge, such as a bear or large predator, may be mistaken for something truly terrifying by the wielder of imagination and fear. Fear, I think, is the main mechanism for warping appearances. It also helps if it's dark out, further blurring the line between reality and imagination. The human mind will supply information where it is lacking, sometimes to devastating effect. This is a common theme in paranormal studies, but that is not to say that every one of these encounters is pure imagination. People have seen truly unexplainable things in the night—with witnesses. In those cases, it is more difficult to attribute a sighting to mere conjecture. Science doesn't dismiss the possibility of unknown entities roaming the earth. Science and the common knowledge only prohibit that these happenings appear all the time. They are anomalies of probability, but just as people somehow win the lottery, the unlucky few come into contact with unknown creatures.

I am going to include encounters with sleep paralysis in this category. It is well known that people encounter strange things when they enter a transitory state between consciousness and sleep but not fully awake. People report seeing "shadow people" at the foot of their beds or silvery entities that surround them and look down. Sometimes, dreams mix with reality, causing the victim to feel a dragging or falling sensation when they are perfectly still. The most terrifying aspect of sleep paralysis is that you can't move as it happens. Thankfully, most instances of these types are over rapidly, like a micro dream. Other times, they can last hours. I believe these types of stories belong here because sleep paralysis is poorly understood. Whatever one experiences during the encounter does not fit with the common knowledge of everyday life. It is unknown whether the entities people report to see are real in some other dimension. Are they psychic vampires come to feed off your fear? Are they some species of alien that can travel between time and space to meet you in your dreams? Some would go as far to say that they are from divine origin. Angels looking after you while you sleep, or some manifestation of God himself. It shouldn't be surprising that many people have reported speaking to God while suffering from sleep paralysis.

The first thing the mind does is try to come up with an explanation. But what does it do when no such explanation exists in plain sight of monstrous terror? Presumably, the mind goes mad. I can only imagine what a failure to compute what is right in front of me feels like—not that I want to know what it entails.

Dog Feeder

My name is Tony. I've been itching to share my story for a while now but I haven't because of fear of being called a liar. But whether or not you believe is irrelevant as I have come to realize in recent times. I'm not scared of sharing what I saw, neither am I afraid of using my first name. There must be at least a billion other people named Tony right? The first thing you should know is that what I saw should not have existed. I believe this creature was a visitor from another world and it somehow got summoned to earth. I base this only on the belief that such things do not exist on earth normally. We have boars, wild dogs, ostriches, elephants, and whatnot—but nothing that resembles what I saw.

My profession is working for Animal Control. I've worked with raccoons, rabid pitbulls, bats stuck in attics and several other nasties for the better of eight years now. I've seen some things, to put it mildly. And yet, everything that I've encountered so far has had a firm backing in what I've known throughout my thirty some years. I know wild animals pose a threat to humans and so have to be dealt with. I know that loose dogs can maul a child to death quite easily, so those have to be dealt with. It doesn't faze me having to put down a rowdy dog. Any mutt or mongrel that poses a threat needs to be eradicated. Many working at the job for almost a decade now has made me a cynic. But if it means protecting the wellbeing of the public, I will do all that is necessary. Usually, I only work emergencies. That in itself isn't saying much, most calls to animal control deal with some sort of crisis—because even an odd bat flying in an attic is the thing of nightmares to poor old ladies living alone.

I remember being called up at five in the morning by a dispatcher. 5 a.m., while early isn't the worst time to call me. I've been giving plenty of sleep by the time I leaped out of bed. If I remember correctly, it was a Friday. The dispatcher told me that a lady called saying that some animal broke into her house and had a run in with her dog. It highly suspected that whatever it was dangerous and probably rabid.

I showed up promptly. The house was only a few minutes away from mine. It felt good arriving at the scene with such swiftness that would make even the police department proud. In any event, when I arrived it was still pitch dark outside. If I had to guess, sunup wouldn't be for another two hours or so. The lady was a few years younger than me, maybe in her mid-twenties and up. She had a kid too, a little boy that was crying beside her. That killed me. Small children are notorious prey for street mutts. I got out my trusty catch pole ready to subdue the attacking animal, which was probably a large dog. As soon as I knocked the woman almost fell on top of me. Boy, was she glad to see me standing there. She kept repeating herself, saying "thank goodness" and "I didn't know what I would do." It honestly was a little annoying.

She quickly explained the situation. She was awoken by loud barking from her Scottish terrier which is when she heard a crashing commotion in the kitchen, as If something was there. How the hell did the animal get inside in the first place? Oh. That's how. Further down the kitchen, there was a sliding door. There was a huge hole in the glass, about 27 inches in diameter if I had to guess. I wasn't about to measure the damn thing. It was huge! There was glass everywhere. It was at that time that I knew it the animal wasn't a god damn dog. It must have been a bear or a cougar. Hell, it could have been some junky from down the street looking to steal something. Stranger things have happened. I will tell you this, no dog no matter how rabid or powerful can break through glass like that. As soon as you close that screen door to the backyard, they will scratch and scratch and bark, but never actually penetrate the damn thing.

Christ. I asked where her dog was and the lady simply pointed outside at the yard with a trembling finger, "It dragged my dog out there," she said with a shaky voice. Uh-oh. Not even a junky would do that. Clearly, it was an animal, probably a mountain lion. Well, I did what any respectable and fearless animal control officer would do at that time. I led with the catcher pole and cautiously made my way toward the yard. I was also packing a tranquilizer gun, just in case. If it was up to me, I'd equip every animal control officer with a .45 caliber pistol. But that's just me. It was very dark out. I could hardly make out objects in the yard except for the dim light coming from the kitchen. I saw what looked like a small tree rustle and upon further inspection noticed that it wasn't a tree. It moved again. There was my mark, whatever the hell it was.

As I got closer my nostrils were engulfed by a putrid smell, like something was rotting. Now, I basically knew the ladies dog was a goner, but even fresh corpses do not smell like that. The thing was double over, moving slightly as if chewing on the remains of the Scottish terrier. I could see the skinny bones on the back of the animal like some emaciated rock star on stage. An Iggy Pop or Marilyn Manson type. Then it started making a terrible noise. A gut-wrenching sound like the type my bulldog at home makes when it's coughing something up. That's what it was doing, in all its gruesome glory. Whatever it was choking on was promptly expelled. Bones, and big ones from the sound of them hitting the floor. Probably a tibia or shoulder blade. I could have turned around then and called for backup, but I didn't. In fact, I know I should have. Instead, I remembered I had a flashlight. Once I produced it the thing I saw before I silenced whatever urge I had to scream.

The thing was no mountain lion I tell you. Nope. What the hell was it? I can only describe what I saw. A huge mouth was immediately recognizable. This thing either had a flexible jaw like a viper's or didn't have one at all because it was unhinged as it sat there devouring the poor little dog. I shone the light too close, and this is when it noticed me. The beast turned its head to face me, revealing the fleshy insides of its mouth and the gaping teeth. It kind of looked like the mouth of a hippo fully agape, but with more incisors. Rest assured, there are no hippos where I live. I could discern no eyes, no ears, no nose or breathing apparatus. This thing was all mouth I tell you! I do believe it was walking on four legs. If you could call those things legs. Never have I seen an animal with such a strange configuration for bone structure. The limbs protruded at almost impossible angles. It looked like an odd spider with only for legs. It let out a bone-chilling growl. "Growl" is the only word I will use to describe it. I've never heard an animal make that noise and sadly, I'm no poet or novelist to even begin to describe the sound.

Stupidly, or perhaps out of fear, I tried to catch the thing with the other end of the catcher pole. I'm no sucker with that pole either. I've been known to grapple charging pit bulls and have them hanging in mid-air seconds later. Well, I got the cursed thing on the first swipe. The strength of the creature was double from an ordinary dog. It tugged, screeched, and eventually I had to let go of the pole because I didn't want to come closer. It charged at me. I instinctually put up my boot to block it, but a for limb caught me, sending a searing pain down my left arm. There was blood. I tried shooting it with the tranquilizer, but I missed. With one final screech and with the pole still attached to what I thought was the neck, the thing jumped over the fence and disappeared.

The poor woman asked me if I was okay. No, I don't think I was okay. Besides the minor scratch on my arm, I was completed jaded. I ended up calling a buddy of mine to the scene and I told him everything that happened. I told him to bring his shotgun. He's the only other person I have told the truth to. I assured the woman a mountain lion came and killed her pet, attacked me and then escaped. It's what I told the guys back at the agency as I called for backup to console the woman further. Somebody would have to dispose of the Scottish terrier's mangled corpse. Thank god it was only the dog that lost its life. I and my buddy drove around until morning came, looking for this damn thing. I don't even know if he believed me at the time, but he was a good friend and saw that I was visibly shaken. I got my armed patched up. I was half expecting a serious infection, but we cleaned it up good. No sight of it. No sight of an escape path or any obvious destruction. We found the catcher pole a few blocks away, which made my buddy a little more sympathetic to my story. The thing must have escaped into the woods or something.

I tell this story not because I seek sympathy but because it needs to be told. Whether or not you believe me, there are things out there that reason cannot explain. I was unlucky. Extremely unlucky to have encountered this creature. You probably won't have such an experience in one hundred lifetimes. But for those who are unlucky like I am, I implore you to understand, so that when you see something that shouldn't be there your shock isn't the same as mine.

Divine Messages

I am someone who has dabbled in the magic arts for a while now. Nothing too crazy, mostly just tarot card readings, burning of sage, that sort of thing. And up to this point, I've never had a mystical encounter, nor have I've taken any psychoactive drugs. I drink coffee regularly, but that doesn't really count. One night I get off from work late and I'm extremely exhausted. I don't eat, don't shower or brush my teeth I just collapse on my sofa and immediately fall asleep. I wake up shortly after, but in a way, I'm still asleep. It's hard to explain, just as any mystical experience is. The common term for it is probably sleeping paralysis except I still had motor control of my body. I felt dead to the rest of the world and at the same time everywhere at once. I immediately sense a presence that was peering at me from the hallway, but I was scared to turn in that direction. I knew I wasn't alone. It started talking to me in a language I didn't recognize but still understood. I thought this presence had to be God, or else an angel because my mind associated the numbers 24 and 16, and for some reason, I thought those two numbers were the most divine.

I said that the presence was in the hallway, but it was everywhere else. It was like I was talking with the universe itself, ever expanding in every direction. I felt like screaming. Once I understood how large the thing was, how it was me, I screamed at the top of my lungs, but nothing came out. I just got sort of dizzy and I felt the presence leave the room. I fell asleep but would wake up in the same fashion multiple times throughout the night. The presence never returned but I had such vivid dreams. I'm not one to believe in religion or the like, but the experience definitely changed my perception of what is possible. I do believe I had a mystical experience and I hope to continue my studies in magic so that I will one day have more such experiences.

CHAPTER 3:
THE MOST CONVINCING BIGFOOT SIGHTINGS

Giants appear all over the world in various different folklores. There is the Yeti or the abominable snowman from Nepal, a large apelike creature with frostbitten fur that lives in the mountains. The North American version is of a nine-foot-tall creature, also described as an ape or hairy man called "Bigfoot" or "Sasquatch." Native Americans have seen this creature and describe it not as an animal, but another type of man. It's an interesting perspective because many believe that humans are descendants of great apes. Bigfoot is described as being ape-like, but it is much larger than any great ape species we currently know about. A possible explanation for Bigfoot sightings is the medical condition called hypertrichosis, a genetic disorder that leaves people with abnormal hair growth just about everywhere on the body including the face. However, these cases are extremely rare, and perhaps rarer still are people who suffer from it and don't actively treat the growth. The explanation also fails because while it can cause people to look like hairy creatures, it doesn't change human proportions. Bigfoot is described as being abnormally tall with ape-like features, and it is unlikely that a human with the condition would be mistaken for it. The condition may be a better explanation for sightings of smaller big feet or hairy creatures that appear to look like Dr. Seuss's Lorax.

The term Sasquatch comes from various Indian names such as *Soss q'atl*, *Sokqueatl*, *Sasq'atl*, and various more. It was coined by a teacher named J.W. Burns who worked at an Indian reservation in British Columbia in the 1920s. Since then, many apelike creatures started being reported in the states, mostly in the Pacific Northwest.

Another question remains of whether or not the bigfoot phenomenon is a hoax. There have certainly been cases of pranksters dressed as ape-men trying to spook people. The tradition can be traced perhaps even further back to when people first started dressing up for Halloween. It then becomes a chicken-or-egg question. Did the legends of big foot come first, or was it people dressing up as apes that started the legend? Until a live specimen is found, this much will always be conjecture. Evidence of Bigfoot is so far confined to the shuttering of old tapes, photographs, and so-called footprints. Sometimes, tufts of hair have been retrieved, only to later be classified as belonging to a bear or wild hog. Some famous audio recordings of two of these creatures communicating can be found online with ease. In the recordings, you can clearly hear wild howls like the ones coyotes make—along with various grunts, yells, and incoherent blabbering that may be some primitive ape language. However, there is no telling if the sounds are legitimate. Look up the "Sierra Sounds" on your favorite search engine, and decide for yourself.

There are countless tapes (arguably each with very bad quality) of an ape-like creature walking around, but because they lack definition, it is difficult to say for sure what is being depicted. Grainy tapes are much easier to fool than high definition ones because the detail is blurred. A man walking with a cheap ape costume would appear as a very convincing big foot on one of these tapes. That no high definition footage has appeared in recent years is telling—especially now that smartphones equipped with megapixel cameras are so ambitious, it is a little odd that no such evidence has surfaced. However, multiple sightings have been reported well into the 2010s, and the legend remains strong. The following stories are based off first-hand encounters with Bigfoot-like creatures. Whether they are the real thing or not is up for debate.

The Backroad Ape

Sometime around 2009, I was studying at a local college in my hometown of Rhinebeck, NY. It's a small town with maybe 7,000 people living there. I actually had to drive to the town over to go to my college. At the time, I was traveling down a back road in Rhinebeck on my way to a performing arts center where I was due for rehearsal. It was a heavily wooded area if I remember correctly. Rhinebeck has many backroads that lead into the countryside. Most of them are abandoned unlike the busy streets in cities. In hindsight, this is probably the best place you want to be if you are an elusive creature. Cars rarely pass by, and when they do they are easy to hear. The woods here are quiet as a tomb.

I was the only car on that road when it happened. I didn't see any cars for a few miles before, so it was unlikely that there would be another witness. But I know what I saw that day. I talked with a few people who live nearby, they all thought I was crazy or trying to prank them. That was until I met an older gentleman, an outdoorsman who frequented hunting grounds nearby. He said he also saw a creature similar to what I described to him. Of course, his wife thought we were both crazy, but it was nice to hear some sort of validation from another person. I do believe there were some species of Big Foot roaming around in that area. Or at the very least, some crazed wilderness man.

Anyways, as I was driving I abruptly came across some bag in the middle of the road and I had to swerve to avoid it. If there was one thing my dad taught me about cars, it's that you have to try your hardest to avoid plastic bags. Those things can stick to the undercarriage of your car, heat up from the exhaust fumes and melt away vital components. I lost control of the car and almost flipped over, so I pulled to the side to inspect for damage. I didn't find anything obvious, but I did notice that the bag had something in it. I walked up to it and saw, to my amazement, an open box of Captain Crunch and a stick. It was a small log, maybe a few inches thick and about a foot long as I walked away from it a saw something from the corner of my eye. It was obscured from view because my car was there, but I definitely saw something move. A figure, about human the size of a human. I thought It was some wino or a local drunk who left their bag there. At any rate, it was somebody I didn't want to be hanging out within the middle of nowhere.

I still had to turn the car around because I sort of spun out. As I was driving away, I got about 50 feet away from the bag when I noticed the figure creep out of the brush. I only got a few second glimpses at it but my god was it large. If I had to estimate, I would say 7 feet at least. It was walking on two feet like a man, covered what looked like black hair. I only got to see it from a side and rear view, but it didn't appear to be wearing any clothes or anything like that. It must have been the fur that covered it. It was large and muscular. The damned thing probably weighed 400 pounds.

The encounter made me feel strange. I was both scared and yet attracted to it. I wanted to learn more. It made me feel a strange excitement knowing that I just saw something absolutely out of the ordinary. But, I didn't want to be late for my rehearsal. It is possible that the mirror made the figure look bigger than what it really was. It could have been a homeless man, but my mind was unconvinced. I've since driven to that place multiple times trying to get another glimpse of the thing, but it's never appeared again.

It Came From the Sandpits

I've lived in the Seattle, Washington area all of my life. It's a great city with plenty of wilderness areas surrounding it. So if you ever get tired of the hustle and the bustle, fresh air and scenic routes are only some 30 minutes' drive away. Back in the 70s and early 80s, I would make frequent trips to Sultan for hunting and target practice. Sometimes I would stay for weeks on end, hanging out a friend's place or renting a cheap motel. If you were a gun aficionado anywhere in Sultan during this time, then you knew all about the gravel pits. Everyone went to shoot there back in the day. This was before the residential areas started popping up near the pits and before the city decided to shut us down. I had made a lot of friends shooting out there, very close friendships I still maintain today. I guess people don't like the sound of guns going off in their backyard. After they closed the pits, we had nowhere else to go for target practice. It was a sad, sad day.

I was down there in the summer of 82' shooting up some targets with my scoped 30-06 Springfield. The pits are a wide and mostly flat clearing in the middle of the wilderness. It's the perfect place for shooting. You can climb on top of a pit and see for a good distance, as I usually day. That day I must have brought at least 100 rounds with me. I had just bought a new clip and I was ready to put it to the test. After taking a few shots at the various targets around the pits, I noticed some movement from the corner of my eye. I shoot with both eyes open. Had one been closed I'm sure I would have missed it. I turned my sights slightly to where the movement came from thinking it may have been a bird, but what I saw instead was a large, brown, woolly thing. I've heard of stories coming out of Siberia of woolly mammoths being spotted in the present day, but this thing was too small to be a mammoth. It was about the size of a man and seemed to be standing upright.

My first inclination was to zoom in with my scope to get a better look. I actually thought it was someone setting up a cardboard target downrange in the middle of my firing. Boy if that were the case I was about to go off on the guy for doing something so stupid. But instead of a cardboard cutout, I saw two glazy eyes that blinked back at me. The thing was standing on top of a pit a little to the left of where I was shooting, so it was about the same elevation as I was. It must have been 75 to 150 feet away from me. As soon as I saw it blink, I knew this thing was alive. That's when I thought, "Bigfoot." One of the most elusive creatures (supposedly) in the world).

I remember someone told me a while back that there are million-dollar bounties on any such creature. I decided then and there to take a shot at it. What other avid hunters wouldn't take it? It was a perfect shot, my rifle still loaded and my sights directly on the things scruffy forehead. Just as I was about to pull the trigger, I hesitated. I would have just as easily mistaken this thing for a guy setting up a target, and I here I was preparing to pull the trigger. I got tunnel vision and lost my situational awareness to the point I felt I had to put the rifle down. I was clearly nervous about shooting it, one because it was so mysterious, and two because I wasn't completely sure it wasn't a person. I just stood there looking at it for another 20 seconds or so before, at last, it turned away slowly and walked away. I immediately ran after it to the spot where it was standing. There was nothing. I spent another 20 to 30 minutes scrounging the area for any evidence of what I saw. Again nothing. No tufts of hair on the branches, no large footprints. I had to estimate the height of the creature with a nearby tree. I marked the area where the top of its head was, and it was some eight feet up the tree. I used my rifle to measure it, holding it up from the butt. I did go back and get an actual tape measure before I left. Eight feet tall.

After almost having shot that thing, I immediately returned to Seattle. I didn't want to be anywhere near the pits. What if it had been a person I saw, and I pulled the trigger? What if it was an actual Big Foot and I shot it? Would the bullet have been enough to even stop it? The implications of catching this thing dead or alive where huge. There would be media coverage surely, and I would be at the center of it all. I don't think I would be the right man for the job. I mean, discovering the existence of a beast from the legend that had gone untouched for hundreds of years? No way man, I'm no Davy Crockett. Just a man with a hobby. I was watching Harry and the Hendersons not too long ago, and the memories came back to haunt me. The thing I saw looked just like that, except maybe not so pretty.

You have to be a special kind of stupid to dress up in an ape costume and appear before a guy shooting rounds from a hunting rifle. So much can go wrong. And if that was indeed a costumed person that I saw, I can only say they did a damn good job at it. There was no smudging of makeup or any obvious sign the thing was a fake. It looked as natural as can be, and that was the scary part. To this day I don't know quite what I saw, but I know that I saw it out there. And no, it wasn't a bear. I've encountered many a bear, even hunted some. This thing was no bear. In retrospect, I'm glad they closed the pits. I've no inclination to go back there anytime soon. I only hope that those who moved into the residential areas don't run into this thing I saw.

Birdshot Man

I never really believed in things like Big Foot growing up. The stories just seemed too fantastical to be any more than stories. My skepticism was only strengthened when I went off to the Uni and every course offered in logic and argumentation. If you are going to be a lawyer, you better be good at defending and attacking arguments. Whenever I hear those types of stories, I have a plethora of logical defenses I can use. Ockham's razor, the burden of proof, several other logical fallacies. I don't preoccupy myself with these things though. In fact, I hadn't really thought about Big Foot since my childhood. That was until I went back home for summer.

This happened in our small town of Blackstone, Virginia back in 2011. My parents owned a respectable house, one that my father practically built from the ground up. They took great pride in owning property and they should have. It was a beautiful house on the outskirts of town. Anyways, I had been there for maybe a few weeks. Everything was as it was before I had left, except my dad had torn down the deck and was working on a new one. He's always working on something despite being retired for a few years now. He told me that they had been hearing strange sounds at night, sort of like a low banging noise against the house. It was most likely a bear that had found some scraps on the side of the house. We also have a cat that my mom loves to death, so a bear was bad news. I knew my way around guns fairly well, even kept a shotgun in my room. Every night I would listen for a little while before falling asleep, but I never heard anything.

But one morning, I was awoken by a loud banging outside. This sounded louder than what my dad had described. I heard him yell at me to get up from upstairs and I immediately grabbed the shotgun and a handful of birdshot shells that I keep in a drawer. Yeah, don't ask. My dad grabbed his revolver I think. We were expecting to see either a large bear or a burglar trying to break in. Either way, I was prepared to shoot at something. Maybe a little too trigger happy. Racing down the stairs I heard a wail, and let me tell you, there's no way a human could have made that noise. It stopped me dead center as I held on to the railing for support. If it was a bear, it was a big one. But I've never heard bears make that sort of high-pitched noise. It sounded like something that belonged in a jungle, rather than in the Virginia woods. I should have realized then and there that something was wrong. Not in the sense that an error was made, but that what we were about to encounter was out of this world.

It was still a little dark outside, but light enough to see. It was that blueish hue you see before the sun breaks through the clouds. At first, I didn't see anything unusual, nor did I hear any more wailing. I searched around the house and especially the deck area for signs of a break in. It was then that my father yelled my name, sounding completely horrified. I turned to his direction where he had been looking out at the woods and I saw it. It was sort of hiding behind tree cover, but there it was. Some seven feet tall, hairy like the Chewbacca character from Star Wars. Teeth blaring and breathing heavily. I could see a cloud of condensation blow with each monstrous heave. It sounded like my Grandpa's old Saint Bernard panting right in front of me. I don't know if it was hungry or what, but the thing looked mean. My dad kept his arm in front of me, but we both had our weapons raised at this point.

"Don't shoot, don't shoot son," my dad told me in the same petrified, stuttering voice from before. "What the hell is that?" For a few moments, we just stood there in the morning dew, staring at each other. The more I looked the more I felt like I would lose my mind. Have you ever stared at a shadow in your room at night that looks like something menacing? Bike handlebars become the horns of the devil, a chair with a towel thrown over it becomes a phantom. It was like that, just staring intently, trying to figure out what constituent parts made up the illusion. Only, this wasn't a shadow in the dark made up of ordinary objects. It was real, breathing, and coming straight towards us.

It took a few timid steps, then it picked up speed. When It was a full sprint, my dad yelled again, "Warning shots!" as if he were giving instructions to a bad guy not to come any closer. It all happened so fast. I heard my dad's pistol go off, and I immediately shot in the air. But I'll be lying If I said I wasn't aiming the bullet spread to slightly hit the charging creature in the face. At the distance we were shooting from, the birdshot surely would have hit the thing. Everything went downhill from there. It let out a scream, probably the most terrible thing I have ever heard. The sound was bad enough, but actually hearing it come out of this things mouth was even worse. Imagine a bear, walking on two legs and yelling "Hey!" at you. You'd be startled too; I don't care how brave you are. It kept charging despite our shots. I knew we landed some, otherwise, it wouldn't have hollered like that.

Instinctually and without saying a word, I and my dad turned our backs on it and ran straight into the house, not once looking back. We immediately looked out the window, and the creature was lost behind a hill. It was nowhere to be seen. We tried other windows but didn't see him. Eventually, we stepped back outside, and it was gone. It left huge footprints, about 18 inches long. But as we followed the trail back to the woods, the footprints stopped. Either this thing climbed into the trees or it disappeared into nothingness. We told mom it was a bear and that we scared it off. The rest of the summer was peaceful. I helped my dad finish the deck and we spent many afternoons barbecuing with family and friends. I and my dad don't speak about it, sometimes when we look out into the woods we give each other this look that says, "Did that really happen to us?" I will never forget the sounds the creature made, nor will I forget the putrid odor that followed it.

CHAPTER 4:

TRUE JERSEY DEVIL STORIES

A chimera is a creature made up of the parts of different animals. One example is the fabled manticore from Persian legends. The manticore has the face of a human, body of a lion, and the tail of a poisonous scorpion. It could be said that the Jersey Devil is also a chimera of sorts, described as having the head of a goat or deer, wings of a bat, and the body of a kangaroo. Sometimes, it is described as having the body of a horse. As the name implies, the legends of the Jersey Devil originate from the seven county-wide regions of forest called the Pine Barrens in New Jersey. This is a large wildlife area famous for its towering pine trees as well as rare species of carnivorous plants. Nobody knows for sure where the Jersey Devil came from. Stories existed of such a creature for centuries, but the prevailing origin story dates to the 1700s.

The legend tells of a woman named Deborah Leeds who lived in Atlantic County in 1735. At the time, birth control was unheard of, and families often reached astounding numbers by today's standards. When Deborah learned that she was pregnant with her thirteenth child, she took it as a bad omen. The number thirteen has always been associated with bad luck and misfortune. She cursed the child not only because it amounted the family headcount to 13 but because she was already struggling to feed everyone. An extra mouth to feed only meant trouble.

When the baby was due, Deborah gave birth to a monstrous creature with red leathery skin. The cursed child resulted in an abomination that resembled something like a kangaroo with horns. It then preceded to slaughter the entire family before retreating into the wilderness of the pine barrens. Locals told stories of shrieking noises coming from the forest at night. When the devil became hungry, it forayed into rural farms and attacked livestock.

Sometime around 1909, the legend resurfaced, as there were reports of a kangaroo-like creature showing up in communities all around New Jersey. In one instance, an entire trolley car of passengers was said to have witnessed it. As it continued its reign of terror, the creature was given its official name, the Jersey Devil. The only means locals had to track the devil was by its distinctive footprints on the snow or sand, said to resemble a two-legged animal with cloven feet. The years following 1909 were largely quiet, as it was believed the devil went back to inhabit the pine barrens for good. However, people continue to tell stories today, and many believe it is still at large.

Similar creatures to the Jersey Devil have been reported in other places. The Sonoran Desert that spans Northern Mexico and the Southwestern United States is home to the legend of the Chupacabras, translated from Spanish, literally meaning "goat sucker." It is described as a dog-like creature, sometimes with wings and leathery skin. The name comes from the belief that Chupacabras feed off of livestock, terribly mutilating them in the process.

Storm Creature

I'm a Jersey native and have sadly lived here my entire life. I keep saying that I will get out of this dump one day, but for now, I just lay low waiting for the day that I can leave. I guess it's not that bad once you get past the high crime areas and run-down cities. The suburbs where I live are actually quite nice. For an added bonus there are beaches just a few hours' drive away. Being from Jersey, I've heard a bunch of different stories about the so-called Jersey Devil that supposedly still lives here. As a kid, I didn't know much about the pine barrens or what those two names meant, and what they had to do with the Jersey Devil, but I still heard them being said quite a bit. It wasn't until my dad took us camping there that I learned it was a perfectly normal forest. Well, I guess the tall pines laid out in rows and columns is a bit unsettling at first. I can understand why stories about the Jersey Devil originated out of this area.

My dad took us camping when I was 12 or 13. I was old enough to know how to use sarcasm, but still a little boy inside. I think because my brain wasn't fully developed at the time I was more gullible to superstitions. At the same time, because I was young I couldn't appreciate the sheer terror of such things if they materialized in front of me. In fact, ever since I made the connection between the Jersey Devil and the pine barrens I went out of my way to look for it on our camping trips. My parents ever the rationalists never had an issue with it as long as I stayed close to the campsite. Sometimes my little cousins would accompany us and I would lead them on monster hunting excursions through the forest, which were always tons of fun but invariably uneventful. I think I found hoof prints once, and that was the closest thing I got to a real sighting.

For this particular camping trip, we took out the RV with us. After countless trips camping out in flimsy little tents and little electricity, my dad decided to buy one. It had everything we needed. Sleeping space, plasma TV, kitchenette even a toilet and shower! The first night there we watched Carrie the movie. It was the first time watching it and I instantly fell in love. I would end up being a big fan of Neil Gaiman and I read all his books growing up. It was just me and my dad for the trip. He slept in the bed at the back of the camper and I had the couch which also pulled out into a bed. I slept directly below the biggest window in the RV but I couldn't look at the stars because my dad pulled down all the blinds that night.

I'm not sure how my dad slept through this but I was awoken in the middle of the night by a loud cracking of thunder. The storm system must have been right on top of our heads, but it was eerie because we double checked all the weather stations before heading out. It was supposed to be a little cloudy, but the chances or rain were a solid 0%. I figured my dad had his earplugs in because after a few cracks I was wide awake, and I couldn't fall asleep again. That's when I made out footsteps in between lightning strikes. It was difficult to differentiate between the noise and the pattering of the rain, but it eventually grew louder and louder. They were definitely footsteps because I could hear the crunch of the forest floor. Boy, was I glad we had brought the RV. If it was an animal, there was no way it could get inside. Still, the sound of footsteps freaked me out. What if it wasn't an animal, and it was a thief or serial killer? The RV was locked and everything, but it was still unnerving as hell. I'm still directly underneath the window so I can look outside if I wanted to. Though at the time I was too scared to really move.

The only light came from the frequent flashes of lighting. Eventually, I braved to look at the curtained window at just the opportune time when lighting flashed and what I saw was the outline of somethings head, staring into the RV. It could have been a shadow and the thing was far away, but since the footsteps were so audible it must have been right up against the RV. The head was elongated, like that of a horse. I made out what looked to be two pointy ears. I'd been trying to fall asleep this entire time, so I was a little groggy. I couldn't really make sense of what I was looking at, much less make a guess of what animal was outside the window. My heart sank when I realized it was indeed an animal because I could hear it making breathing noises on the window. Something a like a big snout dragging itself across the glass. If you have ever been close to a horse, I think you know what I'm talking about. A second powerful lighting strike revealed a mass of something on its head, almost like a Carmen Miranda fruit hat. I gasped. They were tangled-up horns!

The thing, whatever it was, got bored of my window and walked around towards the back of the RV where my dad was. I tried to wake him, but he just nodded off telling me to go back to sleep. I've had trouble with thunderstorms in the past, so that was understandable. Again there was a window in the back and the creature was putting its snout against it making those same horse noises. It got bored of doing that and just started walking away but not before I got a good glimpse of its profile in the window. I could definitely make out two horns twisting off to the side. Its footsteps grew fainter as it approached the camping grounds where my aunt and cousins had their RV. As it left the storm died out with it which was completely bizarre. It was as if a cloud followed it around. In hindsight, if I were a Jersey Devil that's exactly what I would do to mask the sound of my hooves on the ground. I fell asleep quickly after the storm died. The entire encounter couldn't have lasted more than a few minutes.

When morning finally came I jumped out of bed and looked for evidence of its passing. But outside it didn't even seem like it had rained. I failed to find any hoof prints either. I hesitated to share my story with the adults because I knew they wouldn't believe me. I asked my aunt if she saw a horse snooping around the camp and she thought I was crazy. My story was weak because even the tallest horse's head couldn't reach their heads to a window 8 feet up. Unless the horse was that big, which is unlikely. Either the thing I saw was several feet tall, or it was using its hind legs to tippy toe up. Even though we continued going on camping trips to the pine barrens I never saw the creature again. To this day nobody but my younger cousins believes me that I saw the Jersey Devil. I'm still not completely convinced because I didn't see any wings.

Our Little Friend

Back in the 1980s, some of my friends and I took a camping trip in the pine barrens of New Jersey. Prior to this point, I hadn't even heard of the Jersey Devil or any of the other New Jersey folklore. We were just looking for a cool place to camp. I think our ignorance on the matter made the experience a more terrifying one that If we were in the know. Why do I say this? Because if we knew about the stories of such a creature we would at least have some background knowledge to pair with reality. Instead, we had nothing, knew nothing, expected nothing. When strange things started happening we couldn't quantify what was going on. I don't normally believe in hell and demons, but when we were in those woods I felt like we were being stalked by demonic energies. Or at least, that's what my frayed nerves gravitated towards to. Had I known about the Jersey Devil back then, I think I would have still been scared, but not totally freaked out as I was.

We'd all taken our dirt bikes with us to check out some trails. That's another reason why we chose to camp in the barrens, it had some great trails to explore. Getting to the campsite was a little tricky because our unfamiliarity with the area but eventually we found the trails and how they all connected to each other and the campsite. The first night we partied hard, maybe a little too hard because the next morning everyone was either hungover or still a little drunk. Somebody had a grand idea that high adrenaline off-roading would jump-start our systems, so we hit the trails super early. In hindsight that was probably our first mistake. Or I guess you could say that drinking that night had been our first mistake because in our stupor we couldn't reason like we could with a level head. We got a few hundred yards into the woods when all of a sudden, our bikes gave out. They just decided to stall, all of them. One by one we called out that a malfunction had occurred. My good buddy was right behind me. For some reason, he liked to ride close to my ass as possible, something I always hated because we could easily collide if I ever had to break hard. For once, I was glad that he was right next to me. The other guys were separated by maybe 50 feet of wilderness and could only communicate by calling out. "What the hell happened?" I asked him, but he was just as clueless as I was. He thought that maybe the bikes had all taken a beating from the terrain, and simultaneously failed. After all, we were all on the trail for the same length of time. I could see the other guys dragging their bikes towards us through the dense forest. Just as I was about to call out to them, we heard this absolutely piercing scream. It was relentless, getting louder with each scream. We all panicked and ran in the opposite direction in between curses and frantic yells to get out. We were much slower with our bikes still out, but we followed the trail back to the camp. We encountered no one else. Back at the camp, we ask around if anyone else heard the screams. They said they did, up to four miles out from our location.

Our bikes ended up working again. When it got dark we hit the town because we wanted more booze. At this point, I was fine with it because everyone was a little jaded from the previous encounter. We could all use some relaxation. The locals noticed it too because as soon as I sat down the bartender told me I looked as if I saw a ghost. I didn't know what to tell him, but it was late and only a few people were in the bar. Ah, what the hell. I told him everything about our encounter, including the stalled bikes. He took all this with a straight face and he found the stalled bikes extremely interesting. He said he'd never heard that one before. What did he mean by "that one?" Did people often come to this bar with frightening stories to tell? The bartender brushed it off, told me to relax and that I was safe here.

"It sounds like you met our little friend." He invited us all to the back, and none of us decided to follow him. There he showed us an old metallic trashcan, completely shredded to pieces. He showed us the claw marks from which he made the estimate of three claws per shear. "You know what that is boys? That's that Jersey Devil that is." We all filed out of the room listlessly, trying to make sense of what we saw in the confines of our own minds. "So that thing really exists?" one of my buds asked. The bartender said sure, and we sat for a little while hearing him tell the stories. Well, now you know! He said with the biggest grin. I was a little uncomfortable after that, so we bought some beer and left. We decided not to go back to the campsite and checked in to a local motel instead. To be perfectly honest, I never want to go back to that damned forest again.

CHAPTER 5:

TRUE GOATMAN SIGHTING AND STORIES

There are stories out of Maryland about a beast with the hindquarters of a goat and torso of a man. Its fur is matted like a sickly dog and smells of urine and soil. The head exhibits the features of a goat, large pointy ears, and two curved horns. If that wasn't bad enough, the creature stands at a terrifying height of seven feet tall. Legend says that the goatman was the result of a failed human experiment that took place at the Beltsville Research Agricultural Center in Maryland. According to one explanation, a scientist there spliced the DNA of a goat and one of his assistants. Traditionally, human experimentation has been a taboo subject and illegal in most countries, but there are cases of it being conducted by fringe scientists all over the world. Others flee to secret ships in international waters where such laws do not exist. Human cloning has reportedly taken place on such ships. Could it be that such experimentation took place in the research center in Maryland? Whatever the case, there is no mistaking the demonic appearance of the goatman.

The first goatman sighting was reported in 1957 in Maryland where the creature was said to have attacked a group of teenagers in lovers' lane. Allegedly, the goatman uses a hatchet to dismember its victims, which it then consumes. Other cases involve mutilated pets and the sudden disappearance of a group of hikers. Though the goatman has been talked about for decades now, the story remains fresh in the minds of many Marylanders, especially those that reside around Bowie and the infamous haunted Fletcher Road, largely believed to be the goatman's home. Some consider the goatman as nothing more than a teenage prank that has persisted into the modern day, while others still believe it to be the apparition of a devil.

Perhaps the most striking story that came out of Maryland about the goatman was that of a family dog that was found decapitated. Ginger, a German Shepherd mix, belonged to a local family in Bowie named the Edwards until it was found on the side of Fletcher Road—or at least, the head was found. The rest of the body was never recovered. The local police gave the possible explanation that the dog was hit by a train on the nearby tracks and that the head found its way to the road. However, the group of teenagers that found Ginger's head were unconvinced. One of them said that the night before, he encountered a large animal that walked on two legs, had a foul odor, and that made a "screeching" noise before running off. April Edwards, the owner of the dog, also reported seeing a similar animal that walked on two legs the night that Ginger was killed.

The Alabama Shapeshifter

When I was about 16, I went to visit some family in Alabama. I have an uncle who owns a huge tract of land, including several trailers used for hunting and camping down in Huntsville. Being a city boy from Chicago, I looked forward to spending a few weeks out in the bush. Some of my cousins thought it would be a good idea to go camping as soon as I got there. I knew they were all eager to harass me for being a city slicker who didn't grow up on the family farm. I saw a kid not much older than me slaughter a few chickens, pluck them, and quarter them into meal-sized portions. We also brought some bratwurst sausages and drinks and stuffed them all down several coolers. It was going to be a good time. My cousins invited their friends as well. In all, we were ten—six girls and four dudes, all around 15 and 17 years old. What could possibly go wrong with ten teenagers and boozed up in the woods? Of course, at the time, nobody cared about that. We just wanted to have fun with no adult supervision. As we were setting up camp that day, I noticed a strange smell—kind of like copper. I wasn't the only one who smelled it. One of my younger cousins Junior said that it smelled like "ozone." I don't know what that's supposed to mean, but it was a funky smell—sort of like a gassy haze. It sometimes smells like that before electric storms.

I thought nothing of the smell and we all went swimming in the creek rather than unpack our things. We see some rustling in the bush and out comes a white guy carrying a shotgun and his teenage son. I and my cousins are all black, so seeing a redneck looking dude come down the bush like that is more than unsettling. I guess redneck looking dudes are common in the south because one of my cousins started talking to him. Turns out the man is a friend of my uncle lives right near him, and he warned us about some animal lingering in the woods, possibly a cougar. A big animal. We told him we were going to camp for a few days, and he kept saying to be careful. His son named Tanner offered to want to hang with us, which his dad okayed. I didn't mind they both seemed friendly enough. Now there were 11 of us. When the adult left we went back to doing shenanigans, mostly drinking and tossing a football around and telling jokes.

We headed back to the camp to get things in order. Tanner said he wanted to ask his dad if he could camp with us, but it was getting a little dark, so my cousin Rooster said he would go with him, and a girl also went. They had to take flashlights because the sun was about to set and the trail was a good distance out. The rest of us kickback, get a fire going and make some s'mores. It was all fun and games until that weird smell filled my nostrils again. It felt like I had a nosebleed because of the coppery scent in my throat. I go around checking the campsite for any signs of an electrical malfunction. Maybe a hotplate got left on or something. Soon as I'm done checking we hear Tanner and his group running towards us, full speed and absolutely losing their minds. They don't say anything, just go straight into one of the campers and shut the door. We all get this herd mentality and follow them inside, but most of us are laughing like it's a joke. Maybe they saw the boogeyman. Inside it's a different story. Tanner looks honest to god distraught. His face is red as if he'd been crying the whole way here. In fact, he was crying.

I had to tell everyone shut up to let the man speak. This is what he told us: he and the others went to his dad's place to ask for permission which he said yes but warned him again about the animal. Maybe take the rifle, he said. "I saw something in the yard a few nights ago, one of our pigs laid with its guts out and half its head missing. Just left there, like it'd been killed for sport." "We saw something coming back," this time it was Rooster talking. "It was just some guy in the bush making noise. When we shone our flashlights, he was facing away from us and wouldn't turn around." They kept walking on the trail, then they heard low gibbering sounds like if a boar was out there in the bush. "I saw something moving out of the woods," the girl said, also crying. "It was like dragging itself, I don't know what it was." Then Tanner spoke. "Something jumped behind us man, on the track back there. That's why we started running. We saw the light from the fire and booked it in that direction"

 The girls are mostly quiet or still giggling. Some of us are trying to figure out what happened. Maybe some actual rednecks out there messing with us? Possible. The smell of "ozone" was back, this time permeating through the trailer. Everyone already on edge and with that smell reeking, tempers ran short. I was trying to explain to Tanner that if they saw a person then someone is trying to pull a prank. We may even be in real danger. Then out of nowhere, my younger cousin Junior asked: "Did the thing have horns?" What the hell was he talking about? "If it had horns it was probably one of them goatmen. We are probably in his woods we need to get out of here." I told him to stop talking nonsense when everyone is already spooked out. It took some effort to get him to shut up, but eventually, he did, shaking his head all the way.

For some reason, the smell suddenly lifted as if a giant vacuum sucked it right out of the cabin and woods. It was gone as quickly as it had come. I've never experienced a shift in a tactile sensation like that. Usually, when an aroma goes away it fades slowly in varying degrees of intensity, but not this time.

Eventually, people start going back outside to get some fresh air and drink some beers almost as if nothing had happened. I think we were all a little scared at that point and just wanted to get some booze to calm the nerves. It's about 9 or 10 and nobody is thinking about going back home. What if the rednecks from before chased us out of the woods? It was dark—too dark to be traveling in such a large group. Someone could easily fall behind and get lost. Not to mention, I hardly knew any of my cousins' friends. There was Tanner, one of the few white people there. My cousin Junior and Rooster, who I knew very well, and another cousin and his sisters. We did have informal introductions, but I'm not going to lie, some of their names didn't stick well with their faces. I suspected I wasn't the only one who felt this way. We were a little drunk, too. We decided to stay the night, at least, and see what the morning brought.

But nothing else happened. We stay. Some of us still hungover, go to the creek again. By this time everyone has forgotten about last night's events and we are having a good time. I'm getting to know everyone there a little bit better, but at 11 people, it's hard to keep track. I wonder how teachers do it. At around 1 A.M. everyone is huddled around the fire telling stories. Some scary, others just funny. The weird smell comes back, this time so intense that one of the girls doubles over and starts gagging. We go inside, which one provides a little relief. My cousin Junior is piping up about the Goatman again, and how it smells of ozone. I decide it's a good time to fry up the sausages on a hot plate. Maybe the smell will counteract that of the "ozone" and meanwhile we get a bite to eat. This is where Junior accuses me of getting two sausages rather than one. Four to a pack, 3 packs. That's 12 sausages, one each. I only had one sausage. Then it dawned on me. What the hell? Somebody screamed, and everyone ran out of the cabin—as if trying to escape death.

"I counted twelve people in there. Now there's only eleven" said Tanner. How long? How long what? How long where they in that cabin? It's hard to tell. Hell, it could have been in there for that entire day and nobody would have noticed. One of the girls said that someone touched her arm and whispered an indecipherable language in her ear, and that's when she screamed and ran out. It took a great deal of bravery and large sticks to get back inside the cabin. We did another headcount, only 11. Whatever was in here was gone now, that was for sure. The girl who got touched head off the next morning. Three others go with her, including Tanner so he can get his dad's rifle. I had to stay because I had my uncle's keys, and the rest of the group thought someone was just playing games.

We are waiting for Tanner inside the cabin, and someone points out that the girl who was touched is outside. "Look its Keira!" But we had just seen her leave that morning, terrified out of her mind. Then I smelled the coppery smell again. Now people seriously think we are playing a prank on them. I assure them I'm not. One of those girls goes out to get Keira and I just let her go. Let her find out for herself I guess, since words sure as hell aren't working. But before she can get to her, Keira starts acting funny. If I had to describe it, she was extending her back as if laughing, meanwhile bending her knees forward. But there was no laugh. It was dead quiet. The girl bolted right inside after that.

We watch Keira for a while and she just stands there for like 20 minutes. We hear a loud bang on the door that freaks us all out. Then we hear Tanner's voice hollering out to let him in. Keira is nowhere in sight now. Then Tanner says something that throws everyone back into terror. "There are seven people in here. I counted eight earlier" He was right. Whatever that thing was last night had been in here again when we were talking about who was going where. I was glad we had the rifle, though. Tanner told us his older cousin was coming by later to check in on us. A huge argument broke out because people were still accusing us of this thing being a huge prank. We just sit quietly and try to get a station on the radio.

When the cousin shows up, he's confused because Keira isn't with us. "I just ran into her back there I thought she was heading this way. Why was she on the trail, anyway?" He told us how strange she was acting, slowly creeping behind him as he walked, never saying a thing when he tried talking to her. The weird heaving. And he could have sworn she tried saying something to him a low voice, but the words didn't register. "And what's what that smell? Have you guys been frying up pig's blood or what? It got worse as I got to the camp" Slowly I and Tanner tried to get him up to speed with our theory of what was happening. There was the prank theory, and there was the Goatman theory as per my cousin Junior kept reminding us. I don't think the prank theory held any weight now, but the cousin seemed to understand. "It's a good thing I brought my rifle," said the cousin. Now we had two rifles. I was feeling a bit safer.

The smell came back around 11. It was so thick you almost taste blood in the air simply by opening your mouth. Then came the thuds on the door. Half sounding like a banging fist, half sounding like clawing. Then came the voices. "Let me in" Only, the words were stifled, demonic even. Sometimes, cats and dogs make weird noises that owners refer to "talking." It kind of sounded like that. We all sit silently as this continues for a few minutes. The smell fades a little, but we can hear something walking around the cabin, making noise. At about 2 am Tanner's cousin Reese says he's had enough and walks outside with his rifle. He's a bit hysterical, cursing something about "Jesus Christ compels you" he shoots several rounds into the air. We can hear a maniacal hooting in between shots and then agonized screaming as if Reese landed a hit. He ran back inside, and we locked the door behind him. We heard the screams continue until they eventually faded. Whatever that thing was, it probably made its way back to the tree line where Reese had shot it. Slowly, we all nodded off to sleep. Tanner propped a chair next to the door and kept his rifle in his hands. He only told this to me, two days after we left the campsite for good. He told me that he was awoken by someone leaving the bathroom and joining us on the floor for sleep. He said he counted nine people. He pretended to be sleeping but was awake the whole time. He figured if he tried taking a shot, the Goatman would either kill us all, or someone would get hit in the crossfire between two rifles. Instead, he just watched it, opening his eyes every now and then. It left to the bathroom and back several times. It would periodically stand up and heave the same way Keira was doing earlier, or it would start to jitter all over.

Nothing happened in the morning. We all ate breakfast, packed up and were on our merry way. Though this time, nobody was laughing. We had drunk all the booze anyways. Tan caught up to me on the trial and told me that there was a screen-less window in the bathroom nobody had bothered to lock. Of course. That's how the thing got inside nobody bothered to check. I haven't visited Alabama since, and none of my cousins blame me for it.

CHAPTER 6:
HORRIFYING ENCOUNTERS WITH REAL WITCHES

Witches have been a reoccurring theme in the realm of the paranormal since Medieval times. In the present day, stories of witches are told by mothers to get their children to sleep, and rightfully so. Imagine being turned into mice by a coven of witches as told in the 1990 movie *The Witches*. The image of an older mysterious woman in a pointy hat and broomstick is known to every child all over the world. We use terms such as the "witching hour" to describe a period between 3 and 4 am marked by heightened supernatural events.

The Harry Potter series brought renewed attention to the subject of witches, but instead of portraying them as evil creatures, they are given human qualities and the ability to choose between good and evil deeds. Witches get a bad rap, but the literature doesn't support witches as inherently evil. They are mostly misunderstood. Ever since magic entered the human consciousness, there has been a distinction between good and evil—or white and black magic. Historians who specialize in this area talk about an intersection of magic, religion, and witchcraft. Traditionally, the distinction between what is magic and what is religious ceremony has been clouded. Pagan rituals evolved side by side the major religions, and both take influence from one another. What is referred to by paganism is a set of fringe religions that didn't conform to the Judea-Christian ethic. Paganism is a lesser used term today, and the second most common denomination of the word is Wicca, a sort of modern pagan religion. But religion shouldn't be mistaken with witchcraft, which is what this chapter focuses on. Witchcraft refers less to miracles and pagan gatherings and more to the practice or honing or magical abilities. These abilities can range from spellcasting to conjuring curses and benedictions. It also covers the subjects of magical items and potion-making. Other common tropes include divination, shamanism, and tarot card reading.

The history of witchcraft starts with the benevolent. Witches were medicine woman of sorts, who used occult ways to heal people and ward off evil spirits. Sometimes, they did this for a fee, but that is hardly any ground for attributing them to evil. This essentially falls under what is called white magic. It is black magic, or magic intended to cause physical and psychological harm that is seen an evil. Such practices include the manufacturing of curses and conjuring of ill will towards others. Evil witches are seen as sorcerers of artificial misfortune and other such bad things—bad things that eventually lead to the prosecution of witches starting in the 1400s. The so-called witch-hunts were popular in Europe and early American colonies that manifested both as mob violence and judicial hearings. The victims were overwhelmingly young women who, once accused of being a witch, had little recourse. Once branded a witch, they were subject to prosecution by state and local community. Most of the witch-hunt hysteria was fueled by religious intolerance, but there were also cases of mysterious illnesses that had no clear cause or pathology and other misfortunes that seemed to affect those closest to the accused witches.

The common belief is that such "witches" who suffered wrongful prosecutions had little to do with actual witchcraft. That is not to say that the practice of witchcraft doesn't exist. There are stories of real witches, with real magical ability, whether for evil or for good. These witches get less attention because the subject has been clouded by the farcical prosecutions that were the witch-hunts. The line between what is reality and what is accusatory fiction has been clouded. Modern witch folklore isn't about mass hysteria; it is about supposed cases of real witches performing real magic.

Coven

I don't really believe in witches, but after a certain encounter in New Jersey, I changed my mind. I was trekking on the bike trails in the pine barrens with a friend when this happened. We've been visiting the same trails for years and never saw anything out of the ordinary. Me and my friend Steve usually only went in the summertime, but for whatever reason, we decided to go in the early fall when the pine needles litter the floor. At about dusk, it was time to head back to camp so took a little smoking break before turning the bikes around. Probably not the smartest thing to do in a forest full of dead pine needles at your feet but hey, that's life.

One thing you should know about the barrens—when it's warm out there are lots of birds and other forest critters that come out to make noise pretty much at all hours of the day. Everyone is out trying to have sex apparently. Well in the fall and winter time all those animal calls and caws are gone. The forest is so quiet you can literally hear twigs breaking when people step just like in the movies. So when I and Steve are just sitting on this old log enjoying some smokes we get a little uneasy when we hear voices. They were a little far away but voices all the same. They weren't the normal kinds you hear around here, no hollering about to get a sense of location, no drawls of excitement from riding down the trials. No, these voices were hushed, monotone and from the sound of them, multiples. Of course, we had to sit there and finish the cigs, but after we flicked away the buds the voices persisted. I know we both heard them because we both gave each other this look that said: "let's not ignore the elephant in the room anymore."

It was quickly getting darker but we were pulled towards the voices by an intense curiosity, anyone would be. You travel for miles on foot or on a bike with the only sounds heard being the rustling of leaves and then you hear something odd, completely out of place almost. Of course, you want to go and find the source. My first impression was that of a guided tour being held not too far from us but that thought was quickly squashed by the fact that it was so late, and that there were no walking trails this far out.

"Ben!" Steve called my name in the most hushed yet urgent tone I've ever heard any human being use. He was crouching down behind some trees looking beyond a sort of ravine that went to a lower elevation. I thought I'd be seeing some crazed group of college going at it. I couldn't have possibly been more wrong. Below us in what seemed to be 200 yards or so, there was a group of cloaked figures all wearing black. Judging from the many locks of flowing hair most of them had to be women. They were standing in a perfect circle around a pine that looked bigger than the others. I noticed they weren't just talking, they were *chanting*. About twenty of them if I had to guess, with their arms stretched out in front of them towards the tree. It was truly bizarre, especially because the chants were low and their expressions wild. Before either of us could say anything else, the tree ignited in flames from top to bottom. That is, there was no obvious source of the flame. Usually, if you light something the flame travels in some direction. Not this flame. It immediately swallowed the tree as if it had been doused in the propellant. But I didn't see a match being lit. Nobody even touched the tree they were all several feet away from it!

We ran so hard we almost fell over. We mounted our bikes and we were out of there. I didn't fancy being made into a crispy critter like that tree and neither did Steve apparently because he was the first one to bolt. Soon the only thing we heard was the heavy breathing of our lungs and our bike tires running down the trail. And I was worried about causing a fire with my cigarettes! A whole tree burst into flames right in front of our eyes. We never used that trail again, nor did we run into the cloaked women. We never went back there, not even to look for the charred remains of the tree.

Texas Witch

There are real witches out there that exist outside the norms of Halloween personalities and spooky costumes. Real witches are older women that live alone who have long ago abandoned every semblance of normal life. Take it from an old man who experienced such things first hand during his youth and never quite recovered from them. To this day I have nightmares about a certain woman I encountered growing up in Jacksonville.

If you know anything about Jacksonville, you probably know that there isn't much there. Especially growing up in a post-depression era the most you got around here were family farms and liquor stores. It was a small town back then with only a handful of schools, each with only a handful of students. I remember organizing baseball games where half the entire class would show up in a short amount of time to play. Country life was hard but it came with its perks. You learn how to really live and look after yourself. Everyone who grew up with me had this inherent Texas toughness that refused to crack. I guess I wasn't that tough because this witch from my childhood terrified me.

My first encounter with her took place when I was only 10 years old. And yes, it was the same person in later encounters as well. One of the downsides of living in a small town is you can't really get away from people. It's the same old faces, all the time everywhere. I was out playing with my younger siblings having a good old time around sundown. We sort of knew we shouldn't have been out but we were having too much fun to care. I think I'm the only one who saw it, and I remain grateful for that fact. Some couple hundred yards away towards the tree line of the forest I could make out the silhouette of a hooded figure—it was getting dark, and from my vantage point, it looked like it was floating. I kept staring at it trying to get a better look and out of nowhere, it turns its head at an impossible 90-degree angle to stare directly at me. I couldn't tell if it was female or what and I didn't care either. The face made me let out a scream. I quickly round up the kids and ushered them inside where I told my parents the story of a stranger stalking us from a distance. We weren't allowed to play out late after that.

The second encounter happened two years after that and it cost me a friendship. I used to walk to school with the neighbor's boy through a trail in the forest. It was about a 2-mile walk one way, so we sure got our exercise every day. One day we are walking and telling jokes as usual when we pass a stranger covered in quilts pass by us. We couldn't help gawking at this person who was obviously homeless or a bum and who reeked of rotten food and body odor. Something hit me then, some sort of inexplicable stupor that made me feel dizzy. It could have been a type of vertigo from the harsh smell. My friend would later tell me that he felt the same way, sick. I'd never been drunk at that age but I learned a few years later and both felt eerily the same. As we are trying to orient ourselves from the olfactory assault we hear a loud cackling behind us that shakes us to our core. It was the stereotypical witches laugh only worse because we felt lightheaded and confused. I turn around and I see the bum charging at us full speed with arms stretched out. We ran so fast I almost knocked down a door after we got to safety. My friend stopped talking to me after that. I never saw him again; I'd just assumed they took him away somewhere. I don't know why the person in the quilts charged us like that. I was probably harmless, but God was it scary. There's a possibility that the person from this encounter was different from the first and third, but I have sufficient evidence that they were the same person.

My last encounter with the witch occurred many years after. Up to that point, I had no run-ins with witches and such, but I did hear rumors around town about strange happenings. Children were kidnapped, and their bodies never recovered. One of their friends said that they were going to hand out with someone in the woods, but that friend felt something was off and didn't join them. I can only guess this was the witch that took them. I was a senior high school at the time set off to go play football for Oklahoma State. There was a huge (relatively speaking) prom after party in the woods and of course, I went. I say relatively huge because our senior class was maybe 30 or 40 students. Anyways it was quite the party. Everybody was getting drunk and just losing it. I remember looking for this girl who I wanted to get with but had to take a leak instead. I left the general area until I thought it was secluded enough and I did my business. It was at this point that I saw a little smoke emanating from deep in the forest. I thought some knucklehead had set a fire, so I had to check it out.

Well, it was no fire. I didn't have to travel far either. The smoke was coming from a little cottage, probably some hunters camping house. I was glad it wasn't a fire. Except then I smelled the familiar gagging smell from when I was 12. The same smell that gave me vertigo all those years ago. Before I could do anything else a shadowy figure exited the front door, but I couldn't get a good glimpse of the person's face. I heard a hushed voice, what sounded like very fast whispering coming from the figure and I feel a searing pain from my left arm. The damn which was singeing me! Years later I would feel the same pain when getting branded at my fraternity. I had to get away from there before I was just a crisp. The last thing I saw was the figure floating back into the darkness of the woods. I was so far from the party I feared the witch would come after me and nobody would know of my whereabouts. I started screaming for help, simultaneously wetting myself in the process. I blacked out soon afterward and woke in the hospital.

Police ended up raiding the small hut and found all sorts of strange instruments. There were dead animals everywhere like in a hunters tanning studio. Human remains were also found. Nobody doubted that they belonged to the kidnaped children. The witch, however, was nowhere to be seen. I don't know what happened to her or it, but I haven't heard of any witches living in Jacksonville after that. It's likely she or it moved on to the next town to terrify the populace there. I was just glad it was over for me. Even now approaching my twilight years I still remember my encounters with that witch as if they happened yesterday. I keep my home furnished with incense burners and scented candles from bath and body works. I like the smells. I hope I never have to come in contact again with the same rancid stench coming from that hut.

Santeria Grudge

I come from a family that practices Santeria, a sort of religion that originates from the Caribbean. In my opinion, it's less a religion and more a practice of arts and powers given to a select few. Not everyone who follows the religion attains the power of a "santero," which is a title given both to male and female practitioners. I believe Santeria does have white magic applications, but my experiences with it have been mostly bad. A santero is said to have occult knowledge of the world, like some sort of medium that can see into the future and manipulate causality to bring misfortune.

My mother comes from Puerto Rico and my dad from the Dominican Republic. The birthplace is important because these two islands have shared a mutual rivalry for as long as I can remember. Those from Puerto Rico don't get along with those from the Dominican Republic and vice-versa. My grandma on my dad's side is one of these santeros that lives in Miami. People go to her for magical services in exchange for a fee or other gifts. Well, I and our family went to visit her once all the way in Miami. As soon as we stepped through the threshold of the house I could feel the tension in the air between the two. An argument broke out that I forgot what about, but my mom wound up being very disrespectful towards grandma. My dad took her side and they both cussed her out. Then my grandma said something in Spanish that was quite funny at the time, but absolutely terrifying later on. "tu culo se va a podrer y el estomago te va explotar," which translates loosely to "your ass will rot out and your stomach explode." It's a little funnier in Spanish, though. If it's a Spanish saying it's not one I've ever heard. I think it sounded funny because we didn't expect grandma to say such a thing.

She also mentioned that his house would cave in and we would end up living in the streets. My dad laughed in her face because at the ripe age of 30 he was a very successful man. If my parents were worried about what she said they never showed it in front of me. Years passed with nothing out of the ordinary happening, but in the third year, my dad suddenly lost his job. Next, he suffered from medical problems pertaining to the colorectal area. It wasn't cancer, thank god. But a local doctor told us that his condition was on the verge of becoming cancerous. He also needed surgery on his stomach. After a series of floods, the roof in our living room actually did collapse. Eventually, we lost our home after my dad's medical fees and not being able to find a job. We had to live in a shelter for maybe one year. All during this time I kept thinking about my grandma and whether or not our problems were due to her ill will.

My mom was in contact with another santero out of the Bronx. Apparently, both witches knew each other and the lady in the Bronx told my mom that she had disrespected the wrong person, and they had caused our misfortune. On my 17th birthday my mom and grandma made up, and slowly but surely, we started seeing changes in our lives. My dad started a business, and now he's making three times what he did at his last job. His health cleared up and the ailment never reached a cancerous stage. I and my mom have both been blessed with good fortune. I met the love of my life and we are set to get married in a few years.

I'm not sure if I have forgiven my grandma yet. Everyone else has, but I feel that her actions and her enmity were so petty and misguided. What she did was wrong, no matter how I look at it. She often calls home wanting to talk with me, and I dread it every time. I'm never disrespectful to her and I feel that I must answer to matter what. I got in contact with a cousin also on my father's side who lives in the Dominican Republic. They have the same "gift" that my grandma does and she admitted to me that she has cursed people for small infractions. She had even killed people indirectly or caused deaths because of some trivial wrong. Once she told me that a client got angry at her, called the police on her and caused her to miss her morning shopping. My cousin wasn't upset because the police came, but because on her shopping trip that day she foresaw that she would see an old friend and that the friendship would lead to a happy marriage. But she couldn't go shopping that morning because the cops wanted to talk with her. The way my cousin saw it, the small transgression lead to a great infliction of sorrow by missing out on a good life. My cousin cursed the client, and they died a year later in a terrible car accident.

What I learned from all this insanity is that witches are real and can cause bad things to happen to good people. Not only that, but witches are extremely sensitive people. They have capricious tempers and can see so far into the future that a small thing amounts to absolute chaos in their lives. And they do this with little expense to themselves. Nobody can trace a murder that originated as a witch's curse. In fact, it's not even murder at that point. It just is. My advice? Don't ever be disrespectful to a witch. Pay your money on time. Don't complain when their services are not to your expectations. But really, don't involve yourself with them in the first place—that is, if it can be helped.

CHAPTER 7:
THE MIDNIGHT MAN

Somewhere around the early 2010s, a rule for a sleepover game was being spread around internet message boards. It is difficult to tell who the original author of the game is, or what its true origins are. The game is said to be based off an old pagan ritual reserved to punish those that have wronged pagan Gods. In reality, the game sounds more akin to an urban legend. There have been several sleepover games invented in the past used to cause fright. Perhaps most known among these is the Bloody Marry game. The player must repeat "Bloody Marry" for a set number of times in quick succession in front of a mirror. Evoking this name is said to conjure an evil female spirit. Some versions of the game involve the spirit manifesting in front of the player and those who stare for too long get scratched with her claws—or in some cases, killed.

The midnight man is also conjured by player actions, but the process is a little more complicated. First, all the lights inside the house must be turned off. When the hour strikes midnight or directly leading up to it, the player writes their full name on a piece of paper. They are then instructed to douse the paper with a few drops of their own blood. Next, the blood-soaked paper is placed just in front of the front door and a lit candle placed on top of it. The player must then knock on the door a total of twenty-two times, making sure that the hour is exactly 12:00 at the time of the final knock. To let the midnight man inside, the player blows out the candle, briefly opens the door and then promptly shuts it. That is when the fun begins.

The candle is relit, and the player must walk around the house avoiding the midnight man. Some accounts of people playing this game describe the midnight man as a real entity that hides in corners and meshes with the shadows. If the candle becomes unlit, the player needs to relight it at all costs. If they fail to do so, they must step in a circle of salt and remain there until the midnight man leaves. Usually, this happens at 3:33. However, if the player fails to both relight the candle and surround themselves with salt, the midnight man attacks. Hallucinations and panic attacks have been reported at this stage, even bodily harm and the possibility of death. The midnight man must be avoided at all cost. When the midnight man is near, you will know it either by a dramatic drop in temperature or the appearance of a shadowy feature. You may hear things like inaudible whispers. If it comes near you, the player is advised to run.

A Harmless Game

When I moved schools going into freshman year I was lucky enough to make friends with a rich girl. Her name was Annette, she was in the same year as me and had this pretty long flowing brown hair. I was always jealous of her, but she was such a good friend that the jealously never materialized beyond the occasional bad thought. She allowed me to join her friend group right from the get-go and she even introduced me to her family. She took me shopping, bought me presents, and always had my back. I'm not sure how we become so close. I think it was because we both shared a fascination with the paranormal. We could talk for hours about ghosts and the spiritual realm. Both of us had some personal experience in this area and we shared stories all the time.

One day she invited me and another friend to a sleepover at her parent's massive two-story house. Both parents would be gone on a business trip, and we decided we would skip school on Friday to have ourselves a three-day weekend. Milly, the other girl who was invited didn't know me so well but found mutual friendship through Annette. Despite this, she was always friendly towards me. I was super excited to spend an entire weekend at Annette's house with just the three of us. We decided early that no boys would be invited. The plan was to get dropped off at Annette's after school by my Milly's older sister. We didn't tell anyone that no adults would be in the house. I cherished the freedom that my parents gave me early on. If I told them I was going to see Annette they wouldn't protest. If I told them I was going to spend the weekend at her house, they only asked me when I would be back. I knew they were only compensating for the fact that they made us move at such an unfortunate time. Starting off your highs school experience and simultaneously losing all your friends is not something I wish on anyone. I love my parents, despite all their mistakes.

Thankfully I found Annette early in the school year. We first met at PE class. Though she was somewhat popular, she didn't have any friends in our section. We hit it off instantly after we forgot (or refused) to wear our gym clothes and had to sit behind the bleachers while all the other girls ran laps and played volleyball. I don't remember how we arrived at the subject of the paranormal, but before the period was over we were in deep discussion about the existence of ghosts. She told me how she used to spend summers at a haunted cabin owned by her uncle. I told her about how when I was little I would see things. Sometimes I would point at a corner and cry, but everyone assured me there was nothing there. I believe I was seeing spirits, and for some reason being a toddler only I could discern their presence. Before the bell rang, I remember one thing she told me that I probably never will, "These things do exist. And just because science can't prove them, it doesn't mean they are made up."

In a way, we both shared a connection with the paranormal and I thought that was really neat. So did she apparently, because she always treated me better than her other friends. None of them liked talking about the things that we did. They thought it was boring and preferred to talk about boys and fashion. The more I hung out with Annette the more I started noticing about the problems that she had. Despite coming from a well-off family, Annette had frequent mental breakdowns, often over the smallest things. I would be lying if I said they didn't make me feel uncomfortable. I can recall many times I overheard her talking with her parents over her cell phone and how she just seemed to lose control. She would raise her voice and curse a lot. In hindsight, I should have known that she had some anger problems. But when I was with her, I could only smile and think about how cool she was standing up to her parents.

Annette was definitely a risk taker. She had many boyfriends and while I can't say for sure, I believe she slept with all of them. I have reason to believe that some of it took place while we were at school. After all, she would disappear mysteriously in the middle of the school day and I couldn't locate her until hours later. She drank occasionally and would offer me some, which I usually declined. She promised me when summer break came, we would go ghost hunting at her uncle's cabin. It was our strong friendship that allowed me to overlook such things. I was also an impressionable girl, and while I knew that the things she did were wrong, I thought they were kind of cool. I didn't want her to think I was a goodie-two-shoes, so I never told her it was wrong. When she offered me to do things, she simply offered and never pressured me. I really liked that about her.

The day came a few days after Halloween. We didn't get the spend Halloween together, so the sleepover was Annette's way of making it up to me. She promised we would watch spooky movies and play with an Ouija board. I had an uneventful Halloween, so I was completely on board with it all. Milly hung out with us at lunch period and we decided it would be better to ditch for the rest of the day. That felt really good. After lunch, we stocked up on snacks and soda at the vending machines and disappeared beyond the bleachers. It was a big school that had plenty of places to hide. We found a little recess next to an abandoned stairwell. There was a large window and a low wall that if we crouched or laid against it nobody could see us from the other side of the hall. Not that there was anyone to see us there. Whenever we heard footsteps we simply lowered our voices.

For the next four periods, we watched videos on our phones and ate snacks, giggling all the way. We talked about boys and told ghost stories. Annette sprawled on the floor and rested her head on my lap meanwhile Milly laid in the opposite direction with her feet at my shins. It was then that Annette first brought it up. A new game she heard of from a boy, who got it off the internet. Something called the Midnight Man challenge. Annette explained how to set up the game, and then slowly went into detail about how it was played. My immediate thought was that the game sounded really scary and at the same time dangerous. Milly thought it sounded like a good thrill. I said I would do it, but if the midnight man came I wasn't going to stay put. Annette burst out laughing and told me that it was probably a lie, anyway. Whoever heard of a midnight man? We heard a rustling of branches as the big oak outside brushed violently against the lower window. We were quiet for a little bit, then Annette said, "We should play the midnight man game tonight."

The final bang rang, and we all sneaked out of our hiding place to go wait at the schoolyard. In high school nobody really cares if they saw you in the morning but not in the afternoon, only to materialize when it was time to go home. Or else that's what Annette used to tell me. I feel like she was a girl who desperately wanted to grow up. I was just along for the ride. We had to wait for Milly's sister to get off from work, so we hung out on some steps, finishing what was left of our snacks. When the beige corolla finally arrived, the courtyard was hollowed out of students. Only those with extracurriculars lingered about. Every now and then a teacher would pass by. We prayed that our teachers from the classes we skipped didn't go by, but as Annette said, in high school, nobody cares. Milly's sister was also cool. She had tattoos that covered her entire left arm and wore a septum ring. "Are you chicks all ready to go?" She turned the radio to a local rock station that played nu-metal bands of the early 2000s. I felt rebellious, almost grown up.

We made a short stop at Starbucks for sugary drinks and went straight to Annette's house. It was some thirty minutes away, cumulating in a winding two-way street that led us through a forest of autumn trees and other big houses. Annette's house looked ancient. It had a front gate, a cobblestone driveway, a huge porch. I could make out several windows along the two-story structure, and the pointy roofs you only find in rich people's homes. The first time I saw it I couldn't believe my eyes. There were always several cars parked, one of them reserved for when Annette could start driving. "Okay Milly, remember to call your mom later so she won't be on your ass all night. Other than that, you girls have fun." We had all our clothes crammed into our backpacks, so Milly's sister didn't have to help us with that. I half expected her to burn out on her way back, but she drove the Corolla at normal speed.

Annette opened the gate with her personal key and made sure to lock it again before walking us through the house. I've been there a few times and it already felt like a home away from home. My toes curled in anticipation of all the fun things we could do. It wasn't even four O' clock yet and the possibilities were endless. The first we did was a kick off our shoes and socks. Annette turned on the TV and asked us if we wanted something to drink. I think she poured herself some Vodka and mixed it with juice, but I didn't ask for any. The day was spent playing video games, UNO, talking about boys. The usual stuff girls do at sleepovers. I was careful not to eat too much because I really hated using other people's bathrooms. In fact, I think the house had four of them. We jumped outside on her trampoline until sundown.

The night came swiftly. It was hard to believe that some hours ago we were all huddling behind a wall hoping they wouldn't get caught ditching. Annette only kept some lights on the rest of the house was pitch black. Most of our time was spent downstairs in the living room and kitchen. That's where the big TV was. We watched scary movies. Annette kept trying to creep behind us to make us jump, and soon we were doing the same. I think it was after the second movie that Milly fell asleep on the couch. It was just me and Annette. We continued our talk from earlier about ghosts. The subject was on how ghosts can interact with the physical world if they are floating spirits. I said it had something to do with jumping dimensions, but Annette disagreed. She got a little more serious then. She told me that ghosts don't travel through dimensions but that ghosts share our reality. She went as far as to say that they are part of the soul, and insofar as people have souls they also have a personal connection with ghosts.

We put off playing with the Ouija board and instead went upstairs to sleep for the night. Everyone was exhausted from school and then jumping outside. We left some lights on just in case Milly woke up and wanted to come upstairs, but she didn't. Annette told me she would give us a tour of the house when we woke up. So far, I had only seen her room, the kitchen and living room area, two bathrooms and the backyard. I shared Annette's queen size bed that night.

When morning came, Annette was noticeably hungover. We made a quick breakfast and decided to go for a walk to freshen up. It was colder than what we expected. A cold front or something or the other had blown in the night before, and the sky was a deep gray. I thought it was a little unusual. It must have been around noon, but it was so dark outside you'd think that the sun had disappeared. Of course, it wasn't as dark as night, but it was still eerie. Annette told me that ghosts travel with storms. I laughed at the time but walking along the deserted forest made me a little scared. I think the other girls felt it too because we turned back soon after. The rest of the day wasn't as fun as the first, but we still had a good time. Lull's of boredom caused us to retreat to our phones. I had been texting a boy from school and Annette wrote ghost stories. I and Milly giggled nervously as we heard Annette having a breakdown with parents on the phone upstairs. They were worried about her and considered calling someone to look after her. I thought the fun was over, but in the end, Annette convinced her parents not to call her aunt. They didn't know we were there.

Night came and with it, the storm. The rain wasn't falling too hard, but the thunder and lightning were substantial. Annette was set on playing the midnight man game once it got close to 12 o' clock. I was still nervous about it, buy Milly was onboard. They both managed to convince me that it might be fun. I texted my guy friend that we were going to play, and he said to let him know if anything interesting happened. I was totally game after that. Annette couldn't find her Ouija board, so we just lingered about until it was 11. I think we were all a little nervous at that point because nobody said much. Annette gathered everything we needed. We made holes on the top of Morton salt containers for easy access. Three candles were sourced, as well as paper. Annette produced a sharp hunting knife. That scared me. "Netters are you sure?" I had somehow forgotten the blood price requirement in all my excitement. "You don't have to cut yourself if you don't want to," she told me as lightning lit up the backyard screen door. I really didn't want to.

She gave me and Milly the rundown once more. Any room in the house was up to it, but we were to avoid the master bedroom. She'd unlocked the front gate in case someone felt they needed to run out and I guess to let the midnight man in. We all wore our raincoats just in case. Then she did something I wasn't expecting. She picked up our phones from where they were charging and put them in a locked box. "We don't need these until after." I gulped. I still had my nerdy watch, but it didn't have a strong backlight. "Rely on your candles." We were each given a lighter. One by one, we shut off the lights until the living room was the only lit place.

Then we lit our candles and turned those lights off as well. I could hardly see anything except for Milly's anxious expression and the glint of the hunting knife. One by one we wrote our names on the paper. "Now!" I couldn't see it, but Annette had just sliced the tip of her finger. Milly used a needle, I think. I was the only one to put down an unsoiled paper. We started knocking in unison, counting down the seconds. On the 22nd knock, we opened the door and we were engulfed in darkness. The wind from outside had blown the candles out. Frantically we let them back, I heard a shrill scream. Milly. I turned to her and she was smiling. The midnight man was now in the house.

One by one we walked around the spacious living room, candle in one hand salt container in the other. I kept my lighter in my back pocket. We each had big saint candles, they weren't going out anytime soon. I tried to stay close to Annette, but she kept motioning to keep my distance. The first hour or so was uneventful. But with all the lights off you hear things that you normally wouldn't. I think I did hear things move, or else dull thuds coming from upstairs. It was hard to tell with the thunder and rain pelting the old house.

In a way, the storm outside was scarier than the so-called midnight man. I kept checking my watch for the time. Somewhere after 1 is it stopped working. The backlight wouldn't turn on and the digit face was blank. Each girl was in a separate place of the house. I was downstairs still in the kitchen and living room area. I think Milly had gone off upstairs, and Annette was in the garage. My candle flickered off for the first time. I quickly relit it, only to be met by the sound of torrential rain. It was as if the storm intensified as soon as the candle went out. I noticed that the candle continued to flicker, and I panicked a little. I thought I should leave the area and go upstairs. I didn't find Milly. Had her candle gone out already? There was salt all around the shag carpet. I found her in the guest room bath, quivering in fear. She was practically swimming in sweat. I knew we weren't supposed to talk, but she didn't look good. "Where is Annette?" I asked but there was no response.

It's hard to explain what happened next. My initial reaction was to go back downstairs and look for Annette, but my candle went out. I tried lighting it, but the wick was too wet from my sweat. It got cold. Like really cold. But my sweat kept running anyways. I tried running downstairs but found that I couldn't. Like I was in a dream and every time I tried to walk I remained in the same spot. Somehow, I made it to the stairs, which is where I felt the sudden urge to fling myself off them. But, it wasn't me making the decision. I knew it then, that the midnight man was trying to push me off the railing. I poured the salt almost everywhere, creating a solid circle more than a ring. I sat down in a fetal position, not daring to leave. The rain never stopped. The thunder only got worse. I could hear Milly whimpering into the night, but I couldn't move.

I don't know if I feel asleep first, or if I heard Annette's scream before losing consciousness. But I did hear a scream, and a loud wail coming from Milly. I didn't have my watch. My phone was locked. I didn't know the time. But it was Annette who remembered to set an alarm clock for 3:33. I must have spent an eternity clutching my chest on those stairs. I didn't know if Annette was okay. I didn't know if Milly was okay. But I didn't want to risk my life to get to any of them. I knew that as soon as I got up I would fling myself over the stairs. I just knew. It's a decision that I will regret for the rest of my life. I only comfort myself with the contention that at that moment, I was not fully in control of myself. I had lost voluntary action.

When the alarm clock finally went off I practically rolled down the stairs. I could taste salt in my mouth. I ran to Annette by instinct. I thought she would be in the most trouble. When I got to her she was laying down in the downstairs bathroom. I could just make out the glint of a knife. I turned on the lights and saw blood everywhere. I'm not sure how much, but there was a lot. Immediately I screamed. I will never be able to forget the sight of blood congealing on top of mounds of salt. I called 911 and turned on as many lights as I could. I didn't want to touch Annette. I heard Milly come down the stairs also crying. I didn't search Annette for the key to grab my phone. I didn't talk to Milly. I just bolted down the street, screaming.

When the paramedics came they found me on my knees, hands splayed to my sides looking directly up at the sky. I couldn't say a coherent word for 24 hours. We were all rushed to the hospital. Milly suffered from severe bruising and I had a fractured clavicle bone. Annette lost a lot of blood but survived. I was extensively questioned, as was Milly. We all spent at least a few days in a psych ward, suicide watch you name it. We survived, but none of us were the same after that, especially Annette. The official story was that Annette, a girl with a history of mental health issues and substance abuse tried to commit suicide. She even admitted to it. Everywhere we said it was midnight man, Annette said it wasn't. She's been institutionalized ever since. I don't talk to Milly anymore. I spend my days on a high dosage of antipsychotic drugs. I don't know what's real anymore. I am prohibited from trying to contact Annette, and to this day I haven't tried. My parents are thinking about moving away again, to somewhere that doesn't have as much rain.

CHAPTER 8:

THE MOTHMAN

It is difficult to tell what the exact nature of the Mothman is. Some say that it as a psychological apparition of the mind. Others, especially those from UFO circles, believe it to be a type of an alien. Still, some theories have it that the Mothman is an undiscovered species of an animal. Whatever the case, there have been numerous sightings of some "man-like" bird creature usually appearing in the dead of night. Some of the hallmark features of its appearance include bright red eyes and the presence of wings with a wingspan of about 12 feet. The Mothman story originates out of West Virginia in the 1960s where reports were made by multiple people of a flying creature with red eyes.

The first known sighting took place in 1966 when a group of men were digging a grave at a cemetery and were confounded with the appearance of a something large that emerged from the trees and grazed them overhead. A string of sightings continued throughout the following year. Though reports of the Mothman fell sharply after 1967, it has become one of the most famous creatures in American folklore. In those years, sightings of the creature were common. This period is sometimes referred to as the "Mothman phenomena" by fans of the paranormal. Why did the Mothman suddenly appear in 1967 in a small West Virginia town, and why has the image of the Mothman persisted into modern times? Nobody can really say, but for many, Mothman is out there. Variations of the story exist in other places besides the Midwest where most sightings took place. In fact, the presence of some large birdlike creature is common in stories dating back to the Sumerians and in other ancient civilizations as well. The Navajo also tell stories of a mysterious bird creature.

Some do believe the Mothman to be a messenger from beyond, sent to earth to warn people of disasters. Not long after the first slew of sightings in Virginia, the Silver Bridge that connects Point Pleasant, West Virginia to Gallipolis, Ohio collapsed, resulting in the deaths of 46 people. Two victims were never found, but several people reported seeing some large flapping creature in the sky on the very same day. That happened in 1967, near the end of Mothman sightings coming from the Point Pleasant area. Mothman-like creatures have also been sighted in other places of the world directly preceding serious disasters. Allegedly, Mothman was spotted in the weeks leading up to the Chernobyl nuclear meltdown. When the twin towers were attacked in 9/11, people saw a strange smoky figure emerging from the corner of the towers. Many believe it to have been Mothman.

If you are ever in Point Pleasant, West Virginia, you can experience the modern Mothman craze for yourself at the annual Mothman festival. There, you can see the towering 12-foot statue of a man with moth wings erected in honor of the famous stories. There is even a museum dedicated to Mothman and several souvenir shops selling Mothman memorabilia. Some say that Point Pleasant was relatively unknown until the movie *The Mothman Prophecies* was released in 2002. The extra attention led to an influx of Mothman-related tourism that still persists until this day.

Night Hunter

In the winter of 2017, there were several reports of some creature of the night that was about the size of a man but that had sprawling wings like a moth. And by several, I mean upwards of 55. Now I'm not one to think about such things being real, but such a high number in a span of a few months doesn't sound right to me. Either some pranksters were out and about trying to scare people, or there was a collective psychological anomaly that was causing people to see things. I remember the weeks leading up to Christmas I was joking with some buddies of mine about there being something in the water that was causing people to trip out. Maybe some micro-doses of LSD or another psychoactive drug? Hell the CIA has been known to do worse things. The most likely explanation though was a large owl that flew into the city and was causing a ruckus among the townsfolk. Unlikely, given how spread-out reports were and given how big the city was.

This happened in my hometown of Chicago, a place known for many things but not the paranormal. Besides some high-profile UFO sightings in the past, Chicago hasn't really been on the map for that sort of thing. I've always figured UFO guys and so-called paranormal researchers didn't want to come to my city because of the high crime rate. I sure don't blame them. If you show up with one of those bulky cameras to certain neighborhoods, consider it a liability. Cats will steal anything around here, and not hesitate to shoot you either. Some people were saying that the "aliens" had come back, this time in the form of a thing with wings. I don't know a whole lot about aliens and the like. I'm an armed security guard for a technology firm in downtown Chicago. There are several, so I won't say the company by name. Despite having worked for them for the better half of a decade, I've not the slightest clue what the hell they do there, and that's probably for the best. If they need armed security on overnight watch, then they must be guarding something valuable on the server racks. I do mostly out security. I have a little post to the side of the building in a nondescript area, but I'm not really allowed inside. I have talked to guys who work on the inside, and they tell me the security inside is even more beefed up. I see pencil neck techies come in and out of that building on the daily but they don't really interact with me.

Anyways, I mostly work evenings and nights. Most crime is supposed to take place when its dark and downtown isn't the safest place you'd want to be at those hours. Sometimes I'd be the only one on duty outside. Occasionally they give me a partner to guard the other side of the building but that's uncommon. I carry my trusty Sig Sauer .45 handgun at all times. I've never had to actually use it, but you never know. When punks get desperate, they get desperate. I've had to step in and tell shady guys there were entering a restricted area on a few occasions, but beyond that not much in terms of intruders. I figure if someone really wanted to burglarize this place they wouldn't be random street toughs. Competition maybe, and at the worst-case foreign actors. And those types generally infiltrate from the inside rather than out, so I was good in that department. Let the folks inside deal with the Ruskis.

Generally, it's a good, stable job. I have to stand for most of my shift and that gets tiring but not much else is asked of me. Sometimes I do get spooked, being outside for prolonged periods of time. I see weird things on the CCTV monitors, but they tell me those cameras are full of glitches. I was on extra alert during the whole "Mothman" scare not because I believed it to be true but because people seemed to be on edge. Don't ask me why to call it security guard intuition. Before this job, I worked as a bouncer in a nightclub and it was during my time there that I learned how to read people. You can generally tell when someone is about to attack just by the way they act. There's a certain look in their eyes, a look that I was seeing more and more in the months leading up to winter. I saw it in the employees leaving the building each evening and in the faces of people walking around downtown. It was like a collective anxiety of something bad happening. In Chicago, a lot of bad things happen every day, but even we don't walk around looking like that on a regular basis.

A few nights before Christmas Eve, I was at my listening post sipping on some espresso, looking over camera footage from the night before. It's not generally required to do every day, but something told me I should look. I had heard a whooshing sound on my previous shift but there had been no wind that night. The building has some thirty cameras outside alone, so I was pretty busy looking through all of them. Now, I know that robbers don't make whooshing noises. I wasn't looking for evidence of trespassers. I wanted to see for myself if there was such a thing as a Mothman, and if it had somehow wound up around my turf. I was expecting to find some big owl any second as I poured over the data, one camera at a time. It wasn't long before I caught a glimpse of something on one of the back cameras. I couldn't see a figure, but the camera definitely went black for a second, as if something had flown right by it. Interesting, I scrounged the next couple of cameras to get the cross view of the footage I saw and there it was. Again, they aren't the best quality, but on camera #25 I could see what looked like a black leg for a few frames. It was just floating off the corner of the camera angle. The rest of the picture was cut off. I can't control the angles of the cameras sadly.

I knew a "leg" didn't belong in that footage. The camera itself was a clear shot of the ground, meaning that whatever the disembodied leg belonged to had to be at a higher elevation than the camera. I'm trained to use Israeli carry (on an empty chamber) but after I saw that leg I cocked a single round in my handgun just in case. I still had several hours left in my shift, and I knew it would be a long night. As soon as I returned to usual position by some little ways off the main entrance to the building I could feel my hairs sticking up. I didn't like that feeling at all, and I've never seen a leg floating in midair like that. It could have been an artifact, but It looked too real. It sure as hell woke me up, to say the least. I patrolled the perimeter of the building like I never did before. I was out there giving it my 100% just to ensure I didn't run into this thing. I was about to go commando style and start poking my handgun in every shadowy corner I saw. But I never drew my gun that night, which is probably a good thing.

I had to slow down the pace because a few hours in and I was already feeling exhausted. The initial terror had worn off to the point where my hairs were no longer sticking up. My feet hurt from walking more than usual. I was about to return to my listening post for another espresso, but then I heard the same whooshing from the night before. It sounded like flapping wings of an eagle, only much larger. I had no choice but to continue on patrol despite my tiredness. I heard a screeching sound that may have belonged than an owl or something, but I wasn't sure. It sounded more menacing. I was making my way towards the back when I heard the whooshing again. As I turned the corner I felt a rush of wind hit my face, like if some NFL linebacker was charging at me. It all happened so fast. I looked up, and I saw black and red. A flurry of feathers, and floating red eyes. I couldn't make out any limbs, but this thing was huge, my size at least (and I'm a pretty big guy) It just flew off behind another building and I could no longer see it. If I was itching to grab my gun, the thing would have been long gone before I got to draw it. I checked the perimeter once more, and I found the remains of a small bloodied animal. It may have been a dog or a feral cat, but I couldn't tell. I had to call animal control to get rid of the corpse. They told me they had never seen that type of carnage. Clearly, whatever had done it was some type of predatory animal, and to be on the lookout for it.

When I reviewed the camera footage for that night, I only saw a blacked-out image. Camera #17 had a clear shot of the corner I went around, and yet right before I show up there is just a black grainy screen like if some type of magnetic interference caused the camera to lose focus. That was the first and last encounter I had with what I believe to be the so-called Mothman. The only explanation is that it was some large hunting bird, but that fails when you take into account the leg and the blacked-out camera. I think I know what I saw that night, right down to the glowing red eyes. The reports of Mothman eventually left the Chicago headlines and everything went back to normal. I still work at the same place, still have no idea what the company does. I tried to retrieve the footage for myself on a USB drive but someone had whipped the backups earlier than they were scheduled to be deleted. I found that really strange, but I didn't ask questions because I actually like my job. It pays the bills. I didn't want to risk losing it, or my security clearance. I'm not technically allowed to download the said footage anyways, as it belongs to the company. It's either long gone now or sitting on some clandestine server somewhere as definite proof of a Mothman sighting.

CHAPTER 9:

POLTERGEIST STORIES

The word poltergeist comes from the German language. It literally means "noisy ghost." As the name implies, a poltergeist is a spirit or entity that usually haunts houses to make things move or break. They have been known to move silverware, to make things float, to shatter glass, and any number of odd disturbances. The way these things unfold is such that a human being couldn't have possibly done the deed, as nobody else was in sight. A common motif to poltergeist cases are involving young girls around the time when adolescence begins to take hold. One theory is that these young women have the psychic ability to move things without knowing it. It can manifest from a history of traumatic events or anytime the girl is subject to undue stress. Girls around this age are renowned for their emotional volatility and risk-taking behavior. Whenever a girl that possesses physic ability is put in stressful situations, things tend to happen.

Other explanations offer the possibility of haunting spirits who, for whatever reason, are stuck on earth to wreak havoc. The interesting thing about these occurrences is that they are told in almost every continent. From the Americas to Japan, there are stories of vengeful spirits who haunt a specific person. The subject of enmity towards the haunted is a subject of much debate among paranormal researchers. Not all poltergeists are out to cause harm. Indeed, very few cases of poltergeist hauntings result in bodily harm, let alone death. Some spirits are thought to be mischievous or there by pure accident. It still doesn't take away from the scary factor of having things move by themselves in the dead of night, nor does it lessen the psychological impact poltergeist activity inflicts on the family of those involved. One thing is for sure—such activity often worsens at the sight or mention of religious paraphernalia.

The Colosimo Haunting

The Colosimo family lived in a modest house in Spotsylvania, Virginia. They had just moved there, and they soon realized that they had gotten more than what they bargained for. Altogether, there was Sheliajean Colosimo her husband Richard and their 11-year-old daughter Lisa. Sometime in November of 1968, the family started noticing strange happenings around the house which persisted for three weeks until the apparition finally left to the other side.

One day the Colosimo's were entertaining a neighbor Sherry Chewning and her daughter. "Why is this room so cold?" asked Sherry as she entered a guest bedroom that felt icy to the touch. "We aren't sure. Our Lisa used to sleep there but had he move to a different room because of the darn temperature. Even in the middle of summer, that room doesn't get any warmer" said Mrs. Colosimo. Upon hearing this, Chewning recalled old exorcism stories about rooms going inexplicably cold when inhabited by spirits. She then asked Mrs. Colosimo for a cross and rosary which were produced without question. "Leave this place at once! Leave and be gone," repeated Sherry while brandishing the crucifix. "It's getting warming in here," observed Mrs. Colosimo with a tang of worry in her voice. "It is indeed! I am afraid to say Sheliajean, I think there is a spirit in your house!"

The women hung the rosary above the bed and left the room to continue their lunch date. Still a little jaded, Sherry implored Mrs. Colosimo to report it to her church before things got worse. It was a difficult conversation to have to say at the least. Not long after, the girls came inside from playing. "Mommy! We saw a red thing from my old room!" said Lisa, the sound of panic unmistakable in her voice. Both women put down their cups and rushed to the same room. "I can't open it!" The room had somehow became locked from the inside. Sherry tried tackling at the doorknob, but it wouldn't budge. Eventually, Mrs. Colosimo was able to jimmy the lock open, only to be slapped in the face by an ice cold wind. "Oh my god!" The rosary crucifix still hung over the bed, but the bottom T shape had been impaled into the drywall. The beads lined up at an angle like the ropes on a suspension bridge.

Her neighbor refused to step foot in the house afterward, but still accompanied her to the church were a priest handed over a vial of holy water to spread around the room. Following the rosary incident, the Colosimo's experienced a number of disturbances in the night. Each time they awoke from a sound or thudding downstairs, the room was locked from the inside. And upon entering was in a state of disarray. Things only got worse. One night, Richard Colosimo jumped out of bed with a rifle in hand, because he heard someone fling upon the backdoor downstairs. Upon entering the kitchen there was a grisly scene. The door had somehow been expelled from its hinges with such force that nails dug into the opposite wall. The room was again locked and freezing cold.

"Lisa, I told you not to touch the windows after you come from playing outside," said Richard one Saturday morning upon finding what looked like hand prints. But his daughter assured him that she hadn't been playing outside that day. She was in her room decorating her dolls. Next smudges started appearing on walls and the kitchen sink, each resembling a human hand. When the back door flung itself off its hinges for the second time, the Colosimo's thought that enough was enough, and so they contacted a priest from St. Patrick Catholic Church in Spotsylvania to bless the house. Neighbors started pouring salt whenever they walked near the house. It was at this time that a family friend decided to contact a psychic. This woman called herself a witch and said that she was experienced in the clairvoyant and tarot readings.

Upon entering the house, the mystic was immediately drawn to Lisa's old bedroom where she exclaimed she sensed "much energy" emanating from the room. The woman paced around the room, touching the bedsheets with her palms and examining the place where the rosary once stood. "He's definitely in here," she said. "He's scared and confused. A young boy, around the age of 17. Soldier. Confederate. Fatally wounded in battle." Mrs. Colosimo stared at her with mouth agape as her husband crossed his arms. The psychic took out an Ouija board and proceeded to communicate with the spirit. There was a rush of static electricity in the room and everyone's hairs were standing on ends. When the psychic straightened up she informed the bemused homeowners exactly what she communicated. "The boy will be on his way now. I told him to seek the light and to go towards it. He thought there was a war going on still. It's not so. I think you will be safe from here on out."

The only problems the Colosimo's suffered from afterward were rumors about an exorcism and the occasional threat to have their house burned. In a public letter to the community published in the newspaper, Mrs. Colosimo addressed the rumors by saying "There are many things that happen to us in our lives that we don't understand," she wrote. "Nor can we just explain them away with simple science or logic. Such an event happened in my home. I gained nothing by telling the truth. My family and I never really thought about the supernatural. But I now feet what happened to us can happen to anyone, anytime, for no apparent reason"

"Yes, there was a ghost in my home. And yes we were living in fear. And we really don't care who does or doesn't believe us. We know the truth. A good conscience is a continual Christmas. I hope this letter can mollify the skeptics, the pranksters, the obscene callers, and the vandals. Please leave me and my family alone."

The San Pedro Haunting

In 1989 a single mother named Jackie Hernandez moved into a new home from LA to San Pedro, California. At the time she was only 23 years old and recently divorced with a two-year-old son and another on the way. If the difficulties with being a single mother weren't enough, Jackie experienced a number of disturbances in her new home. She reported hearing strange noises like voices coming from the attic, household objects moving on their own, floating orbs of light that when she took pictures of returned the image of an old man and even a viscous liquid that seemed to drip from the walls.

Not long after her daughter was born Jackie came face to face with the ghost she believed to have been haunting her, the same old man from the photographs she took. That was when she called in a group of paranormal researchers at the behest of a friend who also experienced strange things whenever they would visit. This is where someone named Dr. Barry Taff comes in, one of the most respected researchers in the field coming out of the Parapsychology research lab in UCLA. Taff brought along a small team to assist in documenting the haunting.

In August of 1989, the research team heard loud banging noises coming from the upstairs attic, at which point photographer Jeff Wheatcraft decided to go up there for himself and see what he could catch on his camera. It is reported that his camera was wrestled out of his grasp by some unknown force and being flung through the air. The liquid that came from the walls was later confirmed to be male blood plasma. The very next month the team was called again, this time by Jackie who was fearing for her life. In one memorable instance, Wheatcraft went back up to the attic to take pictures and seconds later those who stayed behind heard a loud groan, as if from a pain reflex coming from above. Turns out the same force that had wrestled the camera out of his hand had someone tied a clothesline around his neck and was hanging him the attic rafters. There is photo evidence of this attack taken by fellow photographer Gary Boehm in the moments immediately following the scuffle. The photograph is readily found online.

Jackie Hernandez ended up moving to Walden, California following the gruesome attack hoping to get away from the haunting. To her dreaded surprise, the activity continued even in the new house. Once again, the team was called, and they made the trip to Walden to investigate further. This time they brought an Ouija board and they performed a séance to communicate with the spirits present. The spirit responded that he was dock worker who was murdered back in San Pedro. Apparently, Wheatcraft bore a striking resemblance to the killer, and this is why the spirit targeted him. Soon after, Wheatcraft was attacked yet again by being thrust off his chair into mid-air and crashing into the opposite wall. The haunting activity would continue to plague Hernandez for the following three years before stopping abruptly. But the experience had a profound effect on her and Wheatcraft who reportedly was never the same again.

Dr. Taff made the argument that the spirits being conjured in the various houses that Jackie Hernandez moved to were being caused by a supernatural power that was her own doing. In between the stress of moving, being recently divorced and having a second kid on the way, he concluded that Jackie emanated a negative energy that attracted the spirits and caused bad things to happen. Whether or not that was the case is debatable, but the attacks did eventually stop. What is interesting is that the knot fashioned by the entity to choke Wheatcraft was similar to an old knot used by dock workers in San Pedro, meaning that there was some evidence the spirit was indeed a dock worker in its past life.

CHAPTER 10:

ALIEN ENCOUNTERS

Extra-terrestrial biological entities or aliens have a long history in American folklore and elsewhere as well. The idea of aliens first entered the human mythos probably since ancient times when people looked up at the stars and imagined distant worlds. UFOs, in particular, have been reported for centuries, and some contend that they are even mentioned in the bible as the so-called Wheels of Ezekiel. Perhaps the first instance that aliens touched the American mainstream was with the publication of H.G. Well's War of the Worlds in 1897 and the subsequent radio broadcast in 1938 by Orson Welles, which caused mass hysteria from people believing the earth to be under attack by little green men from Mars.

Since then, there have been repeating cases of UFO sightings as well as alleged cases of alien abduction. In 1947, there was a highly publicized weather balloon crash in Roswell, New

Mexico that many now believe to have been a cover-up for an alien spacecraft crash where actual specimens were recovered and studied by the U.S government. Around this time, the infamous area 51 Air Force testing base gained notoriety for alien-related phenomena. Then, in 1961, a rural farm couple claimed to have been abducted by alien aircraft and aliens who they referred to as the "Zeta Reticulans" after the Zeta Reticuli system where they supposedly originate from. The Hill abduction case took place in New Hampshire and was perhaps the first recorded introduction of the alien Grays, an extraterrestrial race known for their large heads and oval-shaped eyes. There has been no shortage of movies, books, and other forms of media published that depict aliens ever since.

Now, the common discourse centers around conspiracy more than fiction. Is the government hiding the existence of such entities from the public? Many UFO researchers say that they are. Val Valerian is one of the top authorities when it comes to alien research, and he published a volume of reports beginning in 1981 called the Matrix series (no, not the movie) each spanning several hundred pages of compiled research. There are electronic versions floating online that are free to download. However, whoever ventures to read them should be warned, as the books contain harrowing details of a government cover-up. Matrix I, published in 1981, goes over the extensive detail of the alien Grays, covering subjects such as cattle mutilations, human implants, and underground facilities. Research these books at your own risk. The following story is based off a first-hand account recorded in Matrix I.

Visitors from the Mojave

This happened during my time as a researcher for a local university. While I was working on my master thesis I was assigned geological field work to be conducted in the mountains of southern Nevada. I tell this story not because I lead a boring life that requires occasional embellishment of the details, but because the things I saw shook me to my core. Any geologist will tell you that our work is exciting enough for the need of embellishment. Surveying rocks, mountains, and desserts are all the excitement that we need. Being a man of science, I believe strongly in empirical methods. I am well trained in the scientific method as well as experimental design. These are well-established methods for discovering the truth, or close enough to the truth that it is accepted as being true. At the end of the day, logic and science are the only sources of truth that humans can rely on. This much I will take to my grave. My only conclusions from this entire experience are that either these methods are flawed, or there are glaring inconsistencies between what we are told and what is actually out there. I have no reason to believe that science is flawed. On the other hand, I have no way to verify that the so-called empirical facts given to us by our leaders and governments are true. I think we are being lied to. The magnitude of that lie will only become more and more apparent as the twenty-first century takes it course. What I tell you today may put me in mortal danger. As far as I'm concerned, I've already passed to the other side.

The mountains of southern Nevada are beautiful. They make up part of the Mojave Desert, one of the driest deserts in North America. I won't tell you the exact location where I was surveying, both because of my research and because I don't think it's safe for people to go near there. Don't go looking out in the desert either. You are not trained to survive there like I am, you wouldn't last very long. I actively discourage anyone from going into the Mojave for whatever reason. The number of operations going on around that area is astounding. If you are smart, you will stick to the cities. You have probably heard of the military base Groom Lake? I guess you might know it by that other name given by the media, Area 51. That base is also located in the Mojave, but the incident happened miles away from there. Well really it was more than a single incident, that cumulated into one big mess. That's all I can really call it, a mess. Believe me, I've tried other words, but what's the point? No word will do it justice unless I tell you it from the start.

When I go on a survey I either go at it alone or with a trusted partner. The company helps from getting bored when you are out camping in the desert. The areas are usually inaccessible by car, so you have to hike a good ten or fifteen miles a day. I had a dog with me too, Sherry. She is no longer in the picture. The point is, on these geological surveys you want to go with someone else or you will lose your mind. I think that's what happened to Earl because he left the program and was never heard from again. To this day nobody has been able to locate him, not the police or his family. Of the times I was out there, I think I spent two long trips with Earl, each lasting around a week at a time, Well Earl refused to go with me after that second trip. Something happened, and he could never find the words to tell me.

The shorter trips where we didn't go far into the desert where easy, pleasant even. Short hikes only, usually no complicated mapping needed. We went in the morning or afternoon to try to get done before sundown. The longer trips though, you had to endure through the nights. Something about the darkness and the desert is unsettling to say at the least. You hear things you probably shouldn't be hearing. You see lights where there shouldn't be any. Being a scientist and a reasonable person overall, I do believe that most of these feelings can be attributed to tricks of the mind. Being out in the field for days at a time, you don't have the luxury of full course meals. Water can be scarce. I do believe that people start imagining things due to a lack of nutrition. That, and the fact that humans aren't nocturnal, your mind is already on edge when the lights go out. Almost as if you are expecting something to be there. It was on one of those nights that we first saw strange lights. I saw them, Earl saw them. Old Sher probably saw them too. This was on the first long trip we had, maybe four days into the excursion. We had returned to camp as usual and set up a little-canned food dinner. I and Earl talked for a bit, I think I had brought a novel to read then we went off to bed.

I was awoken that night by Sher's barking. Normally well-behaved dog, Sher hardly barks at anything, so you can imagine the state I was in getting up from that tent. We were permitted to carry firearms on our trips, just in case some animal caused us trouble or if we encountered a mad person out in the desert. I remember reaching for my revolver before stepping outside. Earl was nowhere to be found. I yelled for his name, but there was no response. Only Sher's distant barking. I wasn't sure how far she'd gone, but at the time it sounded like a quarter mile away. I figured Earl would be with her, so took off in that general direction. I saw the lights before I could see Sherry. It wasn't a plane, that's for damn sure. If I had to describe the color, I would say just plain white or maybe yellow? The kind of lights you see at night. Not stars, these lights were moving. Multiple. At least a dozen of them, each spread out in equal distances. They formed a sort of lattice in the sky, but each was strobing ever so slightly.

My immediate reaction was to go towards them, towards Sher and Earl to figure out what the hell was going on. No matter how fast I ran through the desert shrubbery and rocks, the lights didn't seem to change in configuration. They must have been really high up. By the time I got to Sher, the lights had disappeared. I found Earl not too far away. He didn't look very well. At first, I thought he was on something because he had a hard time responding to my questions. She stopped barking when I got to her, instead she kept to low whines. Boy, was she happy to see me. Earl, on the other hand, was listless. For the next 20 minutes or so we spent walking back to the camp he had very little words for me. "Did you see those lights?", I asked. He said that he did, but to my surprise, he didn't feel like talking about it further. And every time I asked him what he thought they were, he simply changed the subject. I could tell he was disturbed, so I went easy on the questions. He told me Sher had chased off a medium-sized animal, maybe a wildcat and that is why she was barking.

I didn't know if I was supposed to believe him. The rest of the trip was completed uneventfully. No more barking, or strange lights at night. I think neither of us got very much sleep the following nights. We didn't mention it while we were out collecting data. In fact, we became engrossed in our work as never before. There was a point were Earl and I seemed to shadow each other's thoughts and movements like we shared the same thought processes. We are both competent geologists, so this wasn't too surprising. That we didn't talk about the lights was the surprising thing.

Then on the last day, just as we were getting ready to leave, we encountered something strange. Well, I wouldn't say it was out of the realm of possibility, but it was indeed odd. As we were walking back to our camp, we saw a man, maybe around our age—either the late thirties or the early forties, if I had to guess. He wore a t-shirt and jeans, with no sign of field equipment what so ever. That in itself isn't odd. What is odd, though, is that we were hours away from the closest paved road at the time. There was no conceivable way for this man to be there unless he had also been hiking. But if he was hiking he would need equipment, water at the very least. This man didn't have a backpack or anything else on his person. He didn't speak to us. I'm not convinced if he even saw us. I remember saying a curt "hello," but there was no response. He had Asian eyes, you know the little slits they have? Epicanthic fold I think is what it's called. Probably just a tourist going camping with his friends. I wouldn't blame him for not returning the greeting. At 6'2 weighing 240 pounds, I do come off as a little intimidating. Earl is just as big. We reached the camp and our way back to where I parked. We saw nobody else until we hit the highway back home.

I saw less of Earl after that but we remained in touch. The second trip we did not too long after that was completely uneventful. Earl was in good spirits the whole time, talking about his engagement to his fiancée. Sher didn't bark like she did the previous trip, and we saw no lights. But, there were times that I could not account for Earl's location. He disappeared for maybe hours at a time. At one point I was scared he had gotten lost, but he returned to camp just before dark saying he'd run out of batteries on his satellite phone. That was the only strange thing that happened. But again, is that so strange? When I examined his phone, it was indeed out of batteries. When I asked him where'd he gone, he would say he went off to survey a different area so that we could get the job done twice as fast. We didn't see the Asian man. Overall it was a very successful trip.

Something had changed with Earl. He contacted me even less, and I stopped running into him around campus. I talked to his professors, and they all said he was MIA. I never met his fiancée up to this point, but I under one of our professor's digression I looked up his address and paid a visit. What I learned was pure chaos. He'd been missing for two weeks at the time. The finance knew nothing. Earl had told her nothing. The day before he disappeared was a completely normal day. He simply didn't come home from work. The police questioned me extensively, but the university backed me up on my claims. I had nothing to do with his disappearance. The last time I saw him was on campus a few days after our last trip and he seemed fine.

It wasn't until a year passed that anything else happened. This year in fact, not too long ago. I had begun to think that the desert was just that, a dry geographic area. But two months ago, I was assigned another field trip in the same general area. The things I saw there have wracked my mind with unease. I can't do anything now without thinking about what I saw, and I don't know who I am supposed to reach out to. I will be direct as possible, as there isn't much time for me. Extra-terrestrial biological entities exist, and the government doesn't want you to know. I saw them with my own two eyes. I've been in contact with another man who believes me. Ex-military. He says he's personally met them. Personally, I wouldn't want to.

Here is what happened. I was set for a three-day excursion, just me and Sher. Right from the start, I felt like something was wrong. I couldn't recognize any of the geological features even though I've surveyed the same area countless times. My coordinates were probably off, or there was some bug in the software because nothing was where it was supposed to be. It was as if entire rock faces were picked up and placed somewhere else. It happened during the day, maybe around noon but I'm not sure. I was hiking along with Sher and she started barking. I immediately recognized it as the same terrified barking from the other night. There was no animal though, and it was too bright to see any lights from that one night. The barking continued and intensified. It was then that I perceived a human form in the distance. I wouldn't have spotted them if it wasn't for the bright yellow t-shirt they were wearing. They were simply wandering about like they were lost. I looked at them through binoculars, and I was started to see that they had turned around and were looking directly at me. I swear by you, what I saw was the same Asian man from before! This time, upon noticing me, the man sprinted away like a startled animal. Either he wasn't supposed to be there, or I wasn't. For the first time, I was scared in that desert.

I was scared, but also a little angry that the Asian man simply took off in that manner. Was he doing something illegal, I wondered? I did something that to this day, I still regret. I chased after him as fast as I could, but upon reaching a rock formation that he disappeared behind, he was nowhere to be seen. Sher was still with me, visibly upset and whining nonstop. I ignored her for the most part, which was my second mistake that I regret. We walked for a few minutes in the general direction the Asian man left, going behind more rock formations and losing track of my position multiple times. Sher would no longer follow me—I told her it was okay to stay behind and that I would return for her shortly. What I saw next was mind-altering. How I didn't faint on the spot, I will never know. But a mere hundred yards away from me, I saw a group of Asian people scaling down what looked like invisible stairs. Upon better inspection, I saw a strange outline-like glass under water that was distorting the light around the mountain. It seemed the Asian people were coming from the hatch of a large aircraft that had some sort of cloaking technology, certainly nothing our military had.

After I got back to my senses, I was overwhelmed by panic. I really should not have been there. To this day, I don't know if they saw me, but I remember taking off running as damn fast as I could. I didn't go back for Sher, but I did hear her barking in the distance. I remember how it suddenly stopped, and I didn't hear it again after that. I ran until I was heaving with saliva falling from my gaping mouth. Once I was a suitable distance away, I hid behind some bushes and took my satellite phone out. Neither it or my GPS were working. Upon looking up, I saw a large, military-looking black helicopter hovering only a few hundred feet from where I was. I'm not too familiar with military craft, but this one had no insignia. I didn't know if it was Air Force, Coast Guard, or what. If I had to guess, I'd say it was a black hawk. The strange thing is that I didn't hear it coming until it was right above my head. Usually, rescue helicopters can be heard for miles out, but not this one. I thought I was a goner. Unmarked helicopters are bad news, wherever you are. I tried running, but I was completely out of breath, then the craft just turned around and went in the direction where I encountered the Asian group.

Somehow, I made it back to my car. Sher wasn't anywhere to be seen—and I hate myself for doing this—but I figured my life was more important than hers. Later, I would convince myself that Sher would have gladly given up her life to save mine. Of course, I didn't know what happened to her, but I had a feeling she was no longer alive at that point. Then, I perceived a black town car parked not too far from mine—and I froze. A man pulled the window down and looked at me with this icy look. He was wearing dark glasses, so I couldn't make out his eyes—but the look told me, "I know what you saw. If you want to live, you will never tell anyone about this. Even if you do, nobody will believe you." Then, he just sped off, leaving me alone next to my car. I went straight to McDonald's, ordered 3 big macs, and broke down crying inside the booth. I still see black cars following me around. I know I don't have much time left, but I figured telling someone is the least I can do. It is vitally important that this information is passed on.

CONCLUSION

If you have managed to make it this far, thank you for being brave enough to read the true tales of horror that have been compiled here. Not everyone has the stomach to face the unknown. Those that can do so unscathed are even more rare. The small seeds of fear that are planted in the dark have a way of taking root and spreading. That goes double when the seeds come from true stories, and be assured everything that you have read here is someone's personal narration of their all-too-true waking nightmares.

Even though not all of the stories presented here had terrible consequences or even malicious entities bent on harm, it is important to give the unknown and the mystical the respect that they deserve. Don't assume that just because someone had a pleasant encounter with a supernatural creature once that all interactions will end so civilly. Flirting with such a dangerous category of mystery and possible risk may cost more than you are prepared to pay. More often than not, these things have a way of turning out to be a terrifying trauma instead of a happy memory. Sometimes the happy part is just getting to live to another day.

Don't be surprised if you start to notice things after reading this anthology that you used to ignore. Maybe it will be in the way an animal looks at you, or in the way the temperature drops suddenly. Perhaps you'll be aware of a sudden silence, or a certain person that seems out of place. Whatever cautionary signs you pick up on, listen to their warnings. If you don't, those unnerving signs may be the last things you ever experience. No matter how tempted you may be to investigate the supernatural hovering just in the shadows, think twice before you stake your life on it.

The next time a cold, whistling wind blows through the trees, or you smell a strange scent, keep your wits about you. Keep track of who you're with, and pay special attention to that hidden figure lurking just out of sight. Don't shrug off that chilling tingle spreading up your spine. Don't fight that irresistible urge to flee. You never know what is waiting in the depths of the darkness or what malicious creature is planning on making its move. Your senses might just keep you from being on the wrong end of a folktale.

When it comes to the dangers of the unknown, it is typically best to err on the side of caution. The phrase better safe than sorry never had a more applicable situation. No matter where you fall on the skeptic scale, you have to admit that even the smallest possibility of these stories having truth behind them warrants a healthy sense of apprehension. The world and the universe are too large and too ancient to have exposed all of their secrets. All we can do is pick up the breadcrumbs that are left behind as hints in the form of ghost stories, urban legends, and yes, even folktales.

Double check your surroundings, arm yourself with salt, and keep your guard up. You never know what may come around the corner. If you're in the woods, keep your friends close, and your firearms closer. Hopefully these reports have expanded your mind and given you an exciting scare. They might even come in handy the next time you're gathered around a campfire.

Thank you for sharing in our frightful fun! If you enjoyed this collection of true horror stories and supernatural experiences, please leave a review and let me know what you thought of the book.